Waco Showdown

Pace just stood there, his face reddening with fury.

Sheriff Colby Tucker repeated his order. "I said drop your gun belt, Pace! *Now!*"

"There's no way I'm gonna stare through iron bars for a month," the gunslick declared.

He went for both guns. As he did, the sheriff's reflexes sprang to life, and his right hand was a blur as his gun slid out of its holster. Three shots rang out.

One bullet plucked at Colby's left sleeve like an angry bee, another sang past his right ear. Thirty feet away, the gunslinger staggered backward and fell. Half dazed, Colby walked toward the fallen man and stood over him, seeing that the slug from his revolver had drilled Pace's heart. Life had already left the gunslinger.

Holstering his gun with a shaky hand, Colby looked around at the crowd and said, "Get the undertaker."

The Badge: Book 10
Blood Trail

The Badge Series
Ask your bookseller for the books you have missed

THE BADGE: BOOK 10

★

BLOOD TRAIL

★

Bill Reno

Created by the producers of
Stagecoach, Wagons West,
White Indian, and Winning
the West.

Book Creations Inc., Canaan, NY · Lyle Kenyon Engel, Founder

BANTAM BOOKS
NEW YORK · TORONTO · LONDON · SYDNEY · AUCKLAND

BLOOD TRAIL

*A Bantam Book / published by arrangement with
Book Creations, Inc.*

Bantam edition / April 1989

*Produced by Book Creations, Inc.
Lyle Kenyon Engel, Founder*

ISBN 0-553-27847-9

Published simultaneously in the United States and Canada

---

*Bantam Books are published by Bantam Books, a division of Bantam
Doubleday Dell Publishing Group, Inc. Its trademark, consisting of
the words "Bantam Books" and the portrayal of a rooster, is
Registered in U.S. Patent and Trademark Office and in other
countries. Marca Registrada. Bantam Books, 666 Fifth Avenue,
New York, New York 10103.*

PRINTED IN THE UNITED STATES OF AMERICA

KR   0 9 8 7 6 5 4 3 2 1

BLOOD TRAIL

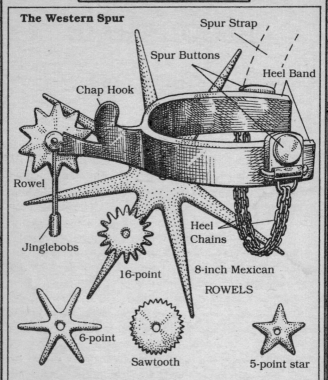

The Western Spur

Spur Strap

Spur Buttons

Heel Band

Chap Hook

Rowel

Jinglebobs

16-point

Heel Chains

8-inch Mexican

ROWELS

6-point

Sawtooth

5-point star

Although spurs were designed to get an immediate response from a horse, most cowboys did not want to harm the animal. The points on most rowels were blunted, and a cowboy who used his spurs to cut the horse was soon unemployed. Originating in Mexico, the spur evolved into two types: those with large rowels, favored in California and Mexico, and those with small rowels, used more often by American cowboys, probably because they could walk without removing such spurs from their boots. Some cowboys added jinglebobs, which provided a kind of music to accompany them as they rode.

RON TOELKE '88

Chapter One

They had a saying at the Texas State Prison in Huntsville that the only successful escapees were the men who had passed through its gates to meet the devil in hell. Some had actually made it outside the somber walls into the fields and forests that surrounded the prison, but the baying hounds and the persistent guards soon tracked them down. Those who foolishly resisted were shot to death; the others were returned inside the walls to face long months of solitary confinement and years added to their sentence.

On a warm sunny day in April 1880, Warden Neal Alton stood at the window of his office and looked down into the prison's exercise yard. Built on one corner of the massive fifteen-foot-high gray wall, the office offered a full view of the yard. It was high noon, and the four hundred convicts were standing in six lines, ready to enter the mess hall through six adjacent doors for their lunch. As he stared at one particular inmate in the second line, Alton growled half to himself, half to the guard standing next to him, " 'Mad Dog' Duke Malone. He sure deserves that nickname. He even *looks* like a rabid dog."

Standing erect in his neatly pressed tan uniform, Harry Blevins nodded. "Yeah. That he does." He paused, observing the tight muscles in the warden's jaw, then said, "Obie must really have had it in for Duke Malone

1

to do what he did. I mean, cutting his hand on purpose so he could get into the infirmary and then come to see you."

Alton grinned, and his pudgy face softened. "How else could Obie have reached me without Malone's suspecting something? They're cellmates, after all."

"Probably no way," Blevins admitted. "Malone's too smart."

"He may be smart," the stocky warden observed with a chuckle, "but he's also a fool. This isn't the first time Gordon Obie has ratted on another inmate."

"It'll sure be his last if Malone finds out."

"He isn't going to find out," Alton coldly responded. "Just to keep any suspicion from falling on Obie, I won't put Malone in solitary until tomorrow."

Blevins pointed through the window. "There's Obie now. Looks like he's heading toward Malone."

Alton and Blevins watched as a small, thin man hurried across the yard to join his cellmate in the line. They could see the two convicts exchange words as Gordon Obie showed Duke Malone his freshly bandaged hand. It was a measure of how desperate Obie was that he had been willing to cut himself badly enough to explain his lengthy absence from his cell.

Obie had lived every moment of his prison life in fear of Mad Dog Malone. Duke Malone had often abused him, Obie had told the warden, and Malone was rumored to be behind at least two killings within the prison walls. Alton had heard the rumors, too, though nothing could be proved against Malone. He could therefore well understand why Obie would want to get even with his cellmate and reveal Malone's escape plan. Having passed other convicts' secrets on to Alton, Obie knew the warden could be trusted. Special favors had been granted to Obie for his tattling in the past, and Alton—being true to his word—had never revealed his source.

This time Obie had been promised that Malone would be put in solitary confinement for five years for planning an escape—by which time Gordon Obie would be a free man. And when Malone finally got out of solitary, he would never be able to prove who it was who had squealed on him, because men in the cells on either side of his own had also heard the killer boast of his plan. Not that it mattered much; Duke Malone was a lifer, with no possibility of parole. He would never breathe free air again, while Gordon Obie would be able to live his life knowing he was rid of the devilish beast forever.

Alton smiled to himself as he watched the guards move the gray-clad inmates into the mess hall single file and the two prisoners passed from view. It was a foolproof plan.

Mad Dog Duke Malone and Gordon Obie stepped out of the harsh sunlight into the mess hall and slowly approached the long table where the food was being served by other convicts.

Duke Malone was of medium height, lean and rockhard with powerful arms and hands. There was a cougarlike fluidity to his movements, and he always looked as if ready to spring on some prey. Even his sharply chiseled features seemed fixed permanently in a cold, feral expression. Those who knew him swore he had been born with the corners of his mouth turned down . . . and with ice water in his veins. His deep-set eyes were as black and hard-looking as marble. Men who had incurred his anger said they could actually feel a physical effect, when he riveted them with his demonic glare.

A thin, white scar ran through Malone's left eyebrow, across the corner of the eyelid, and stopped at his cheekbone. The damaged eyelid had been left with a slight droop, adding to the menace inherent in his face.

On the right side of his neck a broad, thick scar ran in a jagged line downward from his jawline to some unseen point below the edge of his shirt collar. The scars, the deep lines in his face, and the gray that was invading his thinning black hair made him look a decade older than his forty-one years.

One by one the convicts held out their trays and wordlessly accepted food-laden plates and coffee cups from the servers. When his turn came, Malone held out his tray, receiving the usual cup and plate, but then he fixed the server with his devilish black eyes and kept his tray at arm's length, obviously waiting for more.

The prisoner who was serving swallowed nervously and looked pleadingly at Gordon Obie for intervention, but the killer's cellmate looked down at his own tray and said nothing.

Narrowing his eyes, Malone said threateningly, "You want trouble, do you, Ernie?"

Ernie swallowed again with difficulty. "N-no, Duke. But you know the rules. One scoop for each man."

Frowning dangerously, Malone said, "Ernie, you remember Wally Beemer, don't you?"

"Y-yeah, sure."

"You wouldn't like to be in a deep, dark grave like he's in, would you?"

With no further hesitation Ernie took back the plate, piled more food on it, and returned it to Malone's tray. Before Malone could ask, Ernie also gave him a second cup of coffee. The killer was keenly aware that the other men in the line had seen what had taken place, but they all knew better than to say anything.

Duke Malone and Gordon Obie sat down across from each other at a long table and began eating as other men filled in around them. Speaking past a mouthful of beans, the killer asked his cellmate, "So how many stitches did that gash take?"

Gordon Obie had a look of guilt as he answered

nervously, "Uh . . . I think it was nine, Duke. Yeah. It was nine."

"How come it took so long to get your hand tended to, pal? And what are you so nervous about?"

Obie answered quickly, "The doc was out of his office when the guards brought me down there. Took him almost an hour to show up. And I'm nervous 'cause with this bum hand, I won't be able to work as well—and I'm afraid maybe the other men'll think I'm tryin' to shirk my job."

Malone stared for a long moment at the slightly built, middle-aged man whose pasty face was even paler than his colorless hair. Then he nodded, satisfied with the explanation, and shoveled food into his mouth as fast as he could chew and swallow it.

He was just finishing the first helping when guard Harry Blevins stepped up and eyed the mound of food still on Malone's plate and the two cups at his place. The other prisoners looked on with speculation as Blevins said harshly, "How come you've got an extra cup, Mad Dog?"

Malone's face stiffened. He looked up at the guard and said caustically, "It jumped onto the tray, Mr. Blevins. Honest."

Laying a firm hand on the killer's shoulder, Blevins said evenly, "You've been a bad boy, Dukie. You're gonna stay after school. You and me are gonna have us a little talk."

Malone looked up at the man coldly and said through clenched teeth, "Get your hand off my shoulder, or I'll break your arm."

Gripping him more tightly, Blevins waved the heavy riot club in his other hand and retorted, "You try it, and I'll break your stupid head."

Just then the command was given to the convicts to rise from the tables and depart from the mess hall as they had come in, single file. Before leaving the table,

Obie looked at his cellmate and said, "See you later, Duke."

"Yeah, sure thing," Malone said, nodding. "See you later."

Within minutes the mess hall was empty except for the men on kitchen detail. While they noisily carried on with their cleaning, Blevins stood over his prisoner as if he were lecturing him and, amid the clatter of pots and pans, cautioned him: "Make it look good, Malone. Shake your head and wave a hand now and then."

"Yeah, okay," said Malone. "You ready to deal?"

"Only if you've really got money stashed."

"Lots of it."

"If I help you escape, I'll *need* lots of it. I'll have to hightail it out of Texas in a hurry—and I mean permanently."

"You'll have enough."

"How do I know I can trust you, Malone? I mean, maybe after I get you out, you'll decide to do me in and keep all the money for yourself."

Malone shook his head and waved a hand as if in protest. "I'll feel a mighty big debt to the man who gets me out of this hole, Blevins. Believe me, you'll get your share."

The guard cleared his throat and said, "Well, actually, it's gonna take *two* of us to get you out of here."

"Two?"

"Yeah. There's no way I can do it by myself. I've got a plan that'll work, but it'll mean having another guard in on it."

Malone's face screwed tight. "You got somebody in mind?"

"Yep. I've already told him what's in the air without naming you. He's ready to do it."

"Who is it?"

"George Niles."

Malone rubbed his chin and looked at the floor for a

moment. "If you say he's okay, I guess I have to buy it."

"He's okay—hell, he's my best friend. You can trust him. But there's just one thing."

"What's that?"

"We gotta know before we agree to help you how much money you're talking about."

Malone waved his hands, feigning a quarrel with Blevins for the benefit of the kitchen workers, while explaining, "Okay. Here's the deal. I've got fifty thousand dollars buried on the bank of the Red River near Roland. That's not far from Wichita Falls. I'll split it with the two of you. You guys'll get twenty-five thousand and I get twenty-five. How does that sound?"

"Twenty-five thousand dollars!" Light danced in Harry Blevins's eyes. "Okay!"

"And . . . if you two prove yourselves, you won't have to worry about hightailin' it outta Texas. I'll be startin' a new gang. If you come in with me at the start, your cut of all the bank robberies, train heists, and stagecoach holdups will be bigger than what the guys who join later will get."

"Sounds just fine to me," the guard said, grinning. "George will like it, too. We're sick of busting our tails for peanuts in this rathole."

"Good!" exclaimed the killer. "I've been waitin' for six years to break outta this place. Now, what's your plan?"

"Well, it just fell together today," replied Blevins. "Your pal Gordon Obie cut his hand on purpose just so's he could go to the infirmary. While he was getting his hand stitched up, he asked to see the warden."

Malone stiffened. "Why that dirty little—"

Nodding perfunctorily, the guard said, "Yep, that's right. I found out today that Obie's squealed to the warden before. Anyway, he informed Alton right there in my presence that you're planning an escape. I guess you must've told him you had something going—and I sure hope you kept me out of it."

"Don't worry. I didn't tell him it was you I'd been talkin' to. All he knows is I've got somethin' on the cooker."

"He also told Alton that he saw some kind of written list of people you plan to kill when you get out."

"Mm-hmm," Malone confirmed, digging into his shirt pocket. "Got it right here." He laughed humorlessly as he displayed a wrinkled sheet of paper.

"Put that away!" snapped Blevins, looking over his shoulder toward the kitchen area.

Malone complied, then said, "I guess that little rat Obie fits into my escape somehow."

"That's right. See, just so you don't suspect Obie of being the one who ratted on you, the warden is going to wait until tomorrow. Then he's going to have you brought into his office and tell you he's heard a rumor that you're planning an escape. That's all he needs as an excuse to slam you into solitary for five years—and that's exactly what he's planning to do."

Malone swore under his breath.

"So here's the way I've figured it," proceeded Blevins. "I'll arrange for Niles to help me take you to the warden's office right after breakfast. When the moment is right, we'll jump Alton and knock him out, and then tie him up and gag him. I'll tell the guard outside his door that he doesn't want to be disturbed till noon. George and I'll make like we're taking you to solitary, but instead, we'll slip out the east gate to the corral. We'll saddle three horses and leave this place in our dust."

Harry Blevins had known Duke Malone for six years, and he had never once in all that time seen the man smile. He seemed to be waiting expectantly for it finally to happen, since Malone was obviously pleased with the plan and the thought of escaping from prison. For the briefest of moments there was a hint of an upturn to the killer's mouth, but the smile died before it was born as Malone said bitterly, "That mouthy little weasel is gonna get what's comin' to him before I leave this hole."

Blevins shifted uneasily on his feet. "Look, Malone, why don't you just forget Obie? If you kill him, you could mess up this plan. The warden might have you immediately thrown in solitary without talking to you in the office first."

Malone's sharp features distorted with swift rage. "Don't you worry about it, Harry, my friend," he snarled. "I ain't gonna mess up my chances of gettin' out of here. But Gordon Obie is gonna die for shootin' off his mouth, I promise you that. He's gonna die!"

The guard threw a quick glance toward the men in the kitchen. Then looking at Malone again, he said, "Okay, okay, Malone. Just be careful." Pausing, he raised his voice and spoke so the others could hear. "All right, Mad Dog, you'd better see to it that you follow the rules around here, or you'll regret it. Now, let's get you back to your work detail pronto."

That night after the evening meal the prisoners were locked in their cells as usual. Duke Malone was stretched out on his cot and lay with his fingers interlaced behind his head, glowering at the ceiling, while Gordon Obie sat at the cell's small table reading a book by the light of a kerosene lamp. Hatred for Obie boiled within Malone, begging for release. His heart pumped furiously and his muscles tensed, but he restrained himself. He had to wait until lights-out. After the guards had made their final rounds for the night and the prisoners were settled in slumber, he would take care of the dirty little blabbermouth.

As if he sensed his cellmate's fury, Obie placed his hand on his book to keep his place, then twisted around on the straight-backed chair and glanced at his cellmate.

Quietly he asked, "Is there somethin' botherin' you, Duke?"

Malone was staring at the ceiling. Without moving a muscle, he answered, "Somethin's always botherin' me."

"I mean, somethin' different?"

"Just read your stinkin' book," replied the killer in a hard, frigid voice.

Half an hour later the bell rang, the signal for lights-out. Soon all was quiet except for the sound of the guards shuffling through the cellblock, making their final check on the prisoners. Duke Malone lay wide awake on his cot, studying the dim shadows cast on the ceiling by a lantern at the end of the hallway and listening to Gordon Obie's breathing. It was smooth and even. Obie was asleep.

Easing off his cot, Malone stealthily moved across the narrow cell and knelt down beside the sleeping man. Striking as swiftly as a cat, he clamped a hand over Obie's mouth and pounced on top of him. The little man was instantly awake, his eyes bulging. He tried to move, but the killer's strength was too much for him. Breathing hotly, Malone said in a half-whisper, "I trusted you, *friend.* I told you about my escape plans and showed you the list of people I'm gonna kill when I get out. And how did you repay me? You blabbed to the warden!"

A thin whine escaped from Obie's throat as he shook his head and darted his terrified eyes at the cells on each side of them.

"Are you tryin' to tell me that one of the guys in the other cells was the squealer, *friend*?" hissed Malone.

Obie whined again, nodding.

"You're lyin', you little beady-eyed rat! Harry Blevins was in the warden's office when you ratted on me, and he told me all about it. He even told me how you cut your hand on purpose just so you could sneak in and talk to Alton!"

Gordon Obie's eyes bulged wider. Suddenly Duke Malone's fingers closed on his cellmate's throat like steel springs. His thumbs dug into the thin man's protruding Adam's apple, cutting off his breath. Obie struggled, gagging, but to no avail. Gritting his teeth, Malone squeezed until the man's body went limp. Feeling the sweet satisfaction of revenge, the killer then rolled the dead man on his side so that he was facing the wall and covered him up to the neck with a blanket.

Chuckling to himself, Malone returned to his cot and soon dropped off to sleep.

In the morning when Malone rose at the clanging of the wake-up bell, he instantly felt good again at the sight of Gordon Obie's lying dead on his cot. The killer had just finished washing his face with the cold water in the basin when a guard unlocked and opened his cell door.

"Breakfast time," the guard announced, his eyes settling on Obie's still form. "Hey, how come he's still asleep?"

"Sh-h-h!" responded Malone, placing a forefinger to his lips. "Poor guy had a restless night. Cut his hand real bad yesterday, you know. He said he'd skip breakfast this mornin'. He'll probably need to see Doc again when he wakes up."

The guard nodded and locked the cell behind Malone.

Joining the line outside the mess hall, Malone explained to any convicts who asked that his cellmate was not feeling well. Although churning with excitement, he forced himself to be patient as he filed in and got his food, then took it to his usual table.

Just as Malone was finishing breakfast, guards Harry Blevins and George Niles approached his table, announcing in front of the other convicts that Warden Alton wanted to see him. The killer's heart beat faster as he was escorted to the warden's office. This was the day he had been looking forward to for six long years. This was the day he would be free again.

As they made their way up the steps that led to Alton's office, Blevins said, "You pick the time, Malone. Whenever you're ready, we'll train our guns on him so you can knock him out."

"Do we have to do that?" asked Niles. "Why not just let Alton think we're taking Malone to solitary? He won't know the difference till we're long gone."

"Not long enough gone, George," replied Blevins. "What if Alton should tell me to report back to him right after we've locked Malone in solitary? He's always asking me to run little errands for him, and it would be just like him to do that today. Nope, we've gotta do it as I planned. And don't worry, when we tell the guard at the door that the warden doesn't want to be disturbed, the guard won't suspect a thing 'cause that's normal procedure for Alton."

Niles was nodding in agreement as they reached the top of the stairs and saw that Barry Watson was on guard duty. Approaching the door with Malone between them, both guards greeted Watson cheerfully. Then Blevins said, "The warden wants to talk to Malone, Barry."

Watson nodded at his fellow guards, frowned at Malone, and knocked on the door. When Alton answered from inside, Watson pushed it open and said, "Blevins and Niles have prisoner Malone, sir. You wanted to see him?"

"Yes," answered Alton quickly.

Watson stood aside while they entered, and then he pulled the door shut behind them to maintain his post outside the door.

The warden was seated at his desk, which faced the door. Eyeing the prisoner with disdain, he pointed to a straight-backed wooden chair in front of the desk and said to the two guards, "Seat him right there."

Malone dropped onto the chair, flanked by Blevins and Niles, noting as he did so that a file folder bearing his name lay open in front of the warden. There were various other papers on the desktop—as well as a shiny nickel-plated letter opener with a blade an inch wide and eight inches long.

A fly was buzzing noisily against a windowpane behind Alton as Malone gave him an insolent look and asked, "You wanted to see me, Warden?"

Alton regarded the convict with flinty eyes and pulled his lips into a thin slash. Then he angrily upbraided Malone, saying, "You've been a troublemaker ever since you first walked behind these walls. Unfortunately I can't prove it, but I know for a fact that you've murdered at least two inmates since you've been here. And I strongly suspect you've been in on the deaths of three or four others."

Malone grunted, "Like you say, you can't prove it. So get on with your speech."

The warden's face hardened and his neck reddened at the collar. Indicating the papers in Malone's file, he continued, "You're in this penitentiary because you were convicted of killing three people while robbing a bank in Waco—and God only knows how many other people you've killed. If it hadn't been for a soft-headed judge, you'd have stretched a rope six years ago, Malone."

Malone eased back in the chair, folding his arms across his chest. "Did you bring me in here to talk about my past sins, Alton, or do you have somethin' worthwhile to tell me?"

Alton leaned forward on his elbows. "I picked up on a rumor, Malone. The rumor says you're planning a prison break, and that you have a list of people you're going to kill when you get out."

"You and I both know that most rumors don't amount to nothin', Alton. But as a matter of fact, this one is completely true," Malone confirmed. "Whoever gave it to you told it just like it is."

Surprise registered on the warden's face. It was apparent that he had not expected Malone to admit he was planning a break. Alton's surprise increased when Malone produced a slip of paper from his shirt pocket and flipped it toward him, saying, "There's the list. Since you're obviously so curious about my plans, I won't make you guess."

Alton fixed him with a hot glare, then studied the scribbling on the paper. Presently he said, "Five of them, huh?"

"Yep. And all five are gonna die."

Ignoring the boast, Alton looked at the first name on the list. "Marian Daly. There's a Marian listed here in your file—your wife, Marian Malone. Did she take her maiden name back?"

"Naw. She divorced me the minute I was put in this stinkin' prison and then married some wife-stealer named Ted Daly."

"I see. His name is the second one on this list."

"That's right."

The warden's eyebrows rose. "And the third person is the man who arrested you, Sheriff Colby Tucker. I know Sheriff Tucker. He's a fine man."

"The way I see it, Warden," rasped Malone, "he's a *dead* man."

Shaking his head slowly, Alton focused on the next name. "Horace Deming. Who is he?"

"A merchant in Waco. He was foreman of the jury that convicted me of killin' those three people in the Waco Bank. He got real upset when Judge Harwell gave me life in prison instead of hangin' me. Did his dead-level best to talk the judge into givin' me the death sentence. Well, he's gonna get his very own death sentence instead."

The warden merely looked at Malone archly. Then he continued, "The last one is Hans Brummer. And just who is he?"

"He was a member of my gang once. Lower than the scales on a snake's belly, that's what he is. He got arrested first, and then he turned Judas on me. Told Tucker where I was hidin' out in exchange for a lighter sentence. I was sent here for life; Brummer only did a few months in the Waco jail. He's gonna be one sorry bastard, I'll guarantee you that."

Alton folded his arms, leaned back in his chair, and stared fixedly at the killer. His voice was as cold as ice as he said, "You're going into solitary confinement, Malone—and you'll be there for the next five years. Maybe after sixty months in that dark hole you'll sing another tune. If you're still talking about escaping and murdering people then, we'll keep you in there for *another* five years."

The prisoner started to speak when the warden sat forward and reached for a sheet of paper from the file folder. "It's noted on your record that you have a son named Robert, who would now be twenty-two, and a daughter named Libby, who just turned nineteen. Is that right?"

"Yeah."

"Tell me, were you planning to kill your own offspring, too? I mean, if they tried to stop you from killing their mother?"

Malone clenched his teeth and grunted, "I won't let nobody get in my way."

Caustically Alton retorted, "Well, I'm afraid you've got to get out of here first—and there isn't any way you're going to arrange that."

A wicked sneer curled Malone's upper lip. Leaning

forward, he stared icily at the warden's face inches away from his own and said, "Oh, but I already have."

Blevins and Niles took their cue, and Neal Alton's face blanched as the two guards pulled their revolvers and aimed them at him. He looked toward the door as if he were about to call out to Barry Watson, who waited outside.

"Don't do it," Malone warned. "If you call Watson in here, he dies."

Alton licked his lips, his angry gaze going from Blevins's face to Niles's, and he gasped, "What are you two doing? Don't tell me you're going to help this animal escape!"

Malone chuckled coldly. "They're gonna have twenty-five thousand dollars to split between 'em for gettin' me outta here, Warden. And they're gonna get richer yet by bein' charter members in my new gang."

Alton's face reddened as he stiffened and growled, "You'll never get out of here, Malone. There's no way on earth that—"

The warden's words were cut off as Duke Malone struck with the swiftness of a cougar, in one stealthy movement seizing the letter opener and ramming it into Alton's throat. As the killer leaned over the desk, twisting the blade back and forth, Alton gagged, blood spewing from his mouth and neck. He struggled against his assailant for a brief moment, then fell back in his chair.

Leaving the letter opener buried in the dead man's throat, Malone turned to the two guards, who were standing stiffly with expressions of utter astonishment. "Let's get out of here!" he ordered.

George Niles was as white as a ghost. "Good God, Duke, you were supposed to knock him out, not kill him," he said breathlessly.

"He had it comin'!" snapped Malone, striding toward the door. "C'mon. Let's go."

Looking at each other nervously, the guards collected themselves, and they pulled open the office door and emerged with their prisoner between them. George Niles quickly pulled the door shut behind him, and nodding to Barry Watson, he remarked tonelessly, "Warden Alton's got some heavy paperwork to do. He asked me to tell you not to let anyone disturb him till noon."

Watson shrugged and replied, "Sure thing. Whatever the warden wants, the warden gets."

Pretending to escort Duke Malone to solitary confinement, Niles and Blevins moved confidently through the hallways, occasionally upbraiding their "prisoner" for some imaginary infraction. Near the end of one hallway was a supply closet, where George Niles had earlier hidden a civilian jacket that Malone now pulled on. Then, at just the right moment, the two guards and their new leader slipped unnoticed out of the prison into the corral. Hurriedly saddling horses, they mounted up and rode toward Waco, a hundred and twenty miles to the northwest.

Chapter Two

The morning was still quite young as a small crew of men sawed boards and pounded nails, erecting a platform in front of the McLennan County courthouse in Waco, Texas. On hand to supervise the project was Sheriff Colby Tucker, who moved about giving advice to the crew as if his trade were carpentry rather than upholding the law. The workmen had a deep respect for Tucker, so they joked with him and tolerated his directions and interference.

A tall, strapping man, Colby Tucker had just turned sixty, and he was still as strong as a bull ox. His time-weathered face was very handsome, with its thick thatch of silver hair and matching silver mustache, and his pale blue eyes seemed to look right through a person. On many an occasion those eyes had chilled an adversary to the bone, or they had burned his soul with an angry fire.

As Colby paced back and forth giving his unsolicited advice to the carpenters, a slightly built, bookish young man alighted from a buggy and approached him. Watching the young man draw near, the aging lawman held off heading around to the back of the platform.

Stepping up to Colby, holding a pencil and a notebook at the ready, the young man asked, "Sheriff Tucker, may I have a word with you, sir?"

Colby looked at the writing tools and, smiling warmly, asked, "And just who might you be, young fella?"

"My name is Delbert Higgins, sir," replied the young man, returning the smile. "I'm with the *Crawford Sentinel*. You know, from the town a few miles west of here."

"Newspaperman, huh?"

"Yes, sir. Since Crawford is part of McLennan County, we are interested in keeping up to date about our sheriff. My editor, Harvey Naismith, sent me over to get some information on your upcoming retirement."

Tucker pushed his ten-gallon hat to the back of his head and chuckled. "He did, eh? Well, son, Harvey already knows all there is to know—or at least he ought to. We've been friends for twenty-odd years. How long have you been with the *Sentinel*?"

Higgins cleared his throat. "Well, only . . . uh . . . just over three weeks, sir. I came to Crawford from Indiana. A small town called Knox."

"One of those Hoosiers, eh?"

"Yes, sir. You might say that."

Laying a congenial hand on the young man's shoulder, the big lawman said, "Tell you what, my boy. Let's you and me mosey on over to my office. We can sit a spell and I'll tell you anything you want to know." Grinning, he added, "Within reason, of course."

A five-minute walk brought the two men to the sheriff's office. As they walked through the doorway, a lean, rawboned man sitting behind the desk, a deputy sheriff's badge adorning his vest, looked up and smiled. Although his mustache and hair were thick and coalblack, his handsome face was nearly identical to the sheriff's—just a younger version—and when he stood up, he stood exactly the same height as the older lawman.

Removing his hat and tossing it on the desk, Colby said, "Jim, I want you to meet Delbert Wiggins. He's from Harvey Naismith's paper over in Crawford."

Higgins's face flushed as he shook Jim Tucker's hand. "It's . . . uh . . . *Higgins*, sir," he said. "Happy to meet you."

"Oh! Sorry, boy," Colby apologized with a laugh. "Anyway, this is my son Jim. He's been my deputy for the past five years. Since he was twenty-four."

"My pleasure," said Jim. "What brings you here to Waco?"

"Mr. Naismith sent me over to get an interview with your father about his retirement. I . . . uh . . . wasn't living in the county yet when folks voted, but I understand you're to succeed your father as sheriff."

"That's right," the elder Tucker cut in. "In just two days I'm turning my badge over to Jim and letting him take the reins. The intelligent people of McLennan County had the good sense to keep the sheriff's badge pinned to a Tucker."

"Well, sir," said Higgins. "I think that's really wonderf—"

"I've got another son who's a lawman, too," Colby said proudly, interrupting the reporter. "His name's Jeff. He's only twenty-five, but he's marshal of Nacogdoches. You know where that is?"

"Uh . . . no, sir. I don't. I—"

"It's a town about a hundred and fifty miles east of here," Colby informed him. "And I'll tell you what: Both of my boys are outstanding lawmen. Fast and deadly on the draw. And just like their old man, they don't pussyfoot around with lawbreakers and troublemakers. When the people pinned badges on us, we took an oath to uphold the law, and that's exactly what we do."

"I'm sure of that, sir," Higgins declared, nodding. "Could we . . . uh . . . sit down? I think I could write all of this down more easily if I were sitting."

Colby Tucker smoothed his thick mustache and apologized to the young reporter for not immediately offering him a seat. He gestured to the chair beside the large desk, then pulled another one beside it. Slapping his palms against his thighs, the sheriff exclaimed, "Okay, Mr. Wiggins, shoot! What do you want to know?"

"*Higgins*, sir," reminded the reporter quietly.

"Oh, sure," the silver-haired man replied, grinning. "Sorry."

"We're all human, sir," said Higgins.

Jim laughed as he sat back down in his own chair and said, "That's what you think, Mr. Higgins. Dad isn't human—he's Colby Tucker. Any outlaw who ever tangled with him will tell you he's part bloodhound, part mule, part grizzly bear—and part avenging angel. Everything but human."

Colby's pale blue eyes narrowed as he looked at his son. Good-humoredly he declared, "I have a feeling, Mr. Deputy, that when this sheriff's badge is pinned on you, you'll find yourself displaying more animal instincts yourself."

Smiling at their obvious affection and respect for each other, Higgins began to ask his questions. "All right, sir. You seem to be healthy and robust. Would you tell me why you decided to retire?"

"I won't beat around the bush about that, son," replied the weathered lawman. "I'm sixty years old now, and my draw has slowed with age. It's time to step aside before some young gunslick decides to challenge me and I'm forced to draw against him."

"Don't let him kid you," spoke up Jim Tucker. "He's as fast as he ever was. He's just getting lazy. He wants to lie in bed every morning and then play around with his Texas longhorns when he finally does decide to get up."

"You raise longhorns?" queried Higgins, arching his eyebrows.

"Yep. My wife, Edie, and I—we've been married just shy of thirty-two years—figure to take life a bit easier now and make our living raising cattle. We've got a place just outside of town. About two hundred acres of prime grassland."

"How long have you been sheriff of McLennan County?"

Colby scratched his head. "Well, it would've been twenty-three years, come November. But before that I was marshal of Crawford for over twelve years—that's when your Mr. Naismith and I got to be friends—and deputy sheriff here for almost six."

Obviously impressed, Higgins said, "That means you've had nearly forty years of uninterrupted public service as a lawman."

Nodding his head and smiling, Colby said, "That's right—though I was in the Mexican War for a brief spell back in forty-six, till I was wounded. Yep, you might say I've been married to the law far longer than to Edie."

For the next half hour Colby Tucker answered questions about his long career. Higgins probed about arrests made by Tucker, including the names of some of the dangerous men he had put behind bars. When it came to which and how many men he had killed in the line of duty, Colby was reluctant to give any answers. "Let's just say I've put some in their graves, son, but only because I had to. Killing sure isn't something I enjoy. I've always tried to take a man alive if I could—only some men won't let you."

At that moment footsteps were heard on the boardwalk, and suddenly the open doorway was filled with another tall, slender man who might have been Jim Tucker's twin brother if he had not been so evidently a few years younger. He had the same features and the same black hair and mustache. He was even dressed similarly. But in place of a deputy sheriff's badge, a town marshal's star was pinned to the handsome young man's vest.

"Hey!" exclaimed Jim, getting to his feet. "If it isn't Jeff—the black sheep of the Tucker family!"

"What's the saying about the pot calling the kettle black?" chortled Jeff Tucker.

As Jim came striding across the room, Colby got up from his chair and went to embrace his younger son. Then the brothers embraced, slapping each other on the back affectionately. Colby explained to Delbert Higgins that Jeff had come to Waco to attend the ceremony that was to take place in two days at which his father would officially retire and his older brother would become McLennan County sheriff.

Closing his notebook, Higgins thanked Colby for giving him the interview, saying, "I believe I have all I need for my story, Sheriff Tucker. I appreciate the time you've given me, and now I'll get out of your hair so you can enjoy your reunion." After shaking hands with the three lawmen, the young reporter left the office.

The Tucker men gathered around each other, and Jeff Tucker filled his father and brother in on recent events in Nacogdoches, while they apprised him of all that had been happening in Waco. They spent the rest of the morning walking about town, then mounted up and rode north out of town toward the family spread, about two miles from Waco.

Jeff had wired the family as to the approximate time of his arrival, and Edie had planned a big afternoon meal in anticipation of her son's visit. Soon after the three men rode into the yard, the family was arrayed around the large oak table in the high-ceilinged kitchen of Colby's two-story farmhouse, staring at a mountain of food. Seated with Colby, Edie, Jeff, and Jim were Jim's lovely redheaded wife, Nelda, and their two young children, seven-year-old Sam, who was named for his great-grandfather, and five-year-old Susie.

While they devoured the delicious meal the Tuckers talked of old times. Then the subject turned to the event at hand—Colby's imminent retirement and Jim's election as sheriff. Edie, who was a few years younger than her husband, smoothed back a few stray strands of gray-blond hair and grinned. "I guess now I can admit it, Colby: I'm absolutely overjoyed that you're retiring. It will be a big relief to know you're no longer wearing a badge."

Nelda smiled, reached across the table, and squeezed Edie's hand. "Mom," she said tenderly, "you've been a mighty good lawman's wife. I just hope I can be half as supportive of Jim as you've been of Dad."

Colby put his arm around his wife and winked at his daughter-in-law. "Nelda, honey, that's putting a tall order on yourself. This woman is the best. I mean, the very best."

Edie briefly rested her head on her husband's shoulder, then said, "You don't know the number of times though, Colby, when you were off chasing some outlaw, that I wished you did something else for a living. And every time you had a shoot-out with some gun-happy greenhorn who had to test his skills, I thanked the good Lord you came through it alive—but I always wanted to ask you to quit then and there."

Colby pulled her close and told her tenderly, "Why, Edie, I didn't know it bothered you that much."

"Maybe I didn't show it, but I was feeling it. I just didn't want to burden you any more than being sheriff already did."

As Colby kissed Edie's forehead Nelda agreed, "It isn't easy being married to a man who wears a badge, but I know Jim's a born lawman, and he's happy in his work." Turning to smile at her husband, she added, "I love him, and I'll always stand by him. I'm so very proud of him."

The elder Tucker gazed at his daughter-in-law, and his admiration was clearly evident in his expression. "Nelda, darlin', all I can say is Jeff will do well if he

comes up with someone for a wife as good as Jim did."
Turning to his wife, he patted her hand and added, "Of
course, no woman will ever measure up to the one I
have."

"Oh, get on with you, Colby! All these compliments
are going to turn my head," Edie declared, smiling
lovingly at her husband.

"What about it, Uncle Jeff?" young Sam asked abruptly.
"Are you going to get married pretty soon?"

Jeff Tucker laughed ruefully. "Well, Sam, it doesn't
look like it. I've met some nice young ladies, but I
haven't found the one I want to spend the rest of my
life with yet."

"The right one is out there somewhere, Jeff," Nelda
commented, "and one day when you least expect it,
she'll walk into your life."

"I sure hope so," Jeff declared sincerely. "I'm beginning to get mighty impatient."

It was just before noon at the Huntsville prison when
guard Kenneth Gibson unlocked Gordon Obie's cell
and stepped inside. He reasoned that Obie had slept
long enough; it was time for him to go to the infirmary
to have his dressing changed by the doctor. "Hey,
Obie!" called Gibson, standing near the cot and looking
down at the blanket-covered form. "Time to crawl out
of the sack. Doc needs to look at your injury and put a
fresh bandage on it."

When the prisoner did not stir, the guard leaned
down and clamped a hand on Obie's shoulder to shake
him. His hand immediately recoiled; there was no life
in the body. Flinging back the blanket, Gibson swore
when he saw the purple marks on the dead man's
throat. Gordon Obie had been strangled to death, and
there was only one person who could have done it: his
cellmate, Mad Dog Malone.

Gibson immediately went charging out of the cell and

hurried down the stairs, toward the warden's office. Yelling excitedly to Barry Watson, he declared, "Barry, I've got to see the warden! Gordon Obie's dead—strangled! It must have been Malone!"

"Well, no need to worry on that account," the other guard assured him. "Malone's now in solitary confinement, so we know just where to find him." Pulling out his pocket watch, Watson noted, "It's not quite twelve. The warden left strict orders not to be disturbed till noon—but I'll have to interrupt him, with a dead prisoner on our hands." He turned to the door and knocked. When there was no response, he knocked again, calling out, "Warden Alton, Ken Gibson is here! We've got a dead man in one of the cells!"

Watson waited a few seconds, shrugged his shoulders, and turned the knob. Opening the door hesitantly, he peered across the room, then gasped. "Oh, my God!" he whispered fiercely. He flung open the door and rushed into the room, with Kenneth Gibson right behind him.

Gibson felt as though he were going to be sick at the grisly sight of the letter opener, its silver handle glistening in the sunlight, buried in Warden Neal Alton's throat. Barry Watson put a steadying hand on his shoulder, and the two men dashed from the room, calling for assistance.

A quick search of the prison revealed that Duke Malone had escaped and that Harry Blevins and George Niles were missing—as were three horses from the prison's stable. It was presumed that the two guards had aided the cold-blooded killer in his escape. Blevins had been the chief of guards, and now with him gone, Gibson took over. Realizing that the prisoner and the guards had been gone for over three hours, Kenneth Gibson knew it would do no good to take the bloodhounds and try to catch up with them. Federal marshals would have to be called in to take up the chase.

Gibson galloped into Huntsville and sent a telegram to the U.S. marshal's office in Austin, giving details of the escape. Word came back in less than a half hour that two deputy marshals, Clyde Zayre and Lowell Oldham, were being sent to the prison to follow Duke Malone's trail.

Mad Dog Duke Malone and his two companions rode hard toward Waco, keeping to the back country so as not to be seen. When darkness fell, they entered a small town along the way and hid in the alley behind the general store. Late that night, when they were sure that the town was asleep, they crept to the back door of the store and forced their way in. They were able to see clearly enough by the dim light from the streetlamps to keep from knocking into piles of canned goods and other items stacked along the aisles. Keeping their voices to a whisper, the three fugitives gathered rifles and several boxes of ammunition, as well as some beef jerky, cans of beans, and matches. Malone also found a short-handled shovel that he would take to dig up the buried money.

They then hurried to the dry goods section of the store and picked out new clothes, boots, and hats. Malone, after shoving his prison clothing into a satchel, made his way to a display case filled with revolvers and picked out a double-rig holster and two Colt .45s similar to those he had worn toward the end of his outlaw days.

Stealthily leaving the store, the three men secured the rifles and other gear to their saddles, placed the boxes of ammunition in their saddlebags, and rode out of town without being seen. A few miles farther along the trail they came upon an old abandoned barn. After spending the night there, they rose at sunrise and quickly mounted up. They rode hard as they continued toward Waco, which they hoped to reach the following day.

That same day the early morning sun threw a soft yellow light into the Tucker kitchen where Edie cleared the breakfast dishes for her husband and younger son. Rising from the table, Jeff said, "Dad, I appreciate your letting Jim have off this morning so he and I can go fishing. We haven't done anything like this since I left home."

"Glad to do it, Son," the silver-haired man said, smiling. "Besides, not only am I glad to let you boys have a good time, I'm looking forward to a big fish fry for supper tonight."

With fishing poles in hand Jim pushed open the kitchen door, letting a warm breeze into the room. "Ready, Jeff?" he asked.

"I sure am. Let's go. See you later, Dad."

The brothers hurried off, and Colby turned to his wife. Kissing Edie, he said, "Well, it's off to the salt mines for this old boy, honey."

She embraced him and said happily, "Just one more day, and only my two boys will be wearing badges. Oh, Colby, it'll be so nice to have you here puttering around the place, away from all the outlaws, drifters, and gunslingers."

Colby snickered. "You'll probably get tired of having me underfoot after just two days."

Squeezing him hard, she replied, "Would you care to place a small wager on that, my dear?"

Kissing her again, he laughed. "Okay, beautiful. You're on."

Grabbing his large Stetson, the sheriff gave his wife an affectionate wink, then went out to the barn and saddled his horse. Mounting his animal, he rode toward Waco, eager to supervise the decorating of the now-completed platform built for Jim Tucker's induction ceremony as McLennan County sheriff.

After giving explicit instructions to the ladies who were doing the decorating, Colby Tucker headed for his office. He had been hard at work for a few hours, and it was just past eleven o'clock when a middle-aged man burst through the door.

"Sheriff," he said fearfully, "trouble's brewin'! Curt Pace is back in town!"

Tucker's face stiffened. "I told that no-good gunslick to stay out of Waco. Where is he, Walt?"

"Over at the Lone Star Saloon."

"I assume by 'trouble brewing' you mean he's been bragging about how quick he is on the draw, goading others into doing the same."

"Yeah, that's right," Walter Stinn replied. "Billy Ray Halton's gettin' ready to challenge him."

"That fool kid!" Tucker exclaimed, shaking his head as he rose to his feet. "He'll never live to see his twentieth birthday if he doesn't get this gunfighting nonsense out of his system—and the worst man for him to meet up with is Pace." As he dashed through the door, with Stinn following right behind him, he added, "Pace is a seasoned gunfighter, and if Billy Ray is stupid enough to go up against him, Pace'll kill him for sure."

While the two men hurried along the street toward the Lone Star Saloon, Colby asked, "Is Pace alone?"

"Yeah," gasped Stinn, struggling to keep up with the sheriff, whose strides were much longer than his own.

"Well, that's fortunate, anyway," Tucker declared. His face was grim when he reached the saloon. Shouldering his way through the batwing doors, he saw Curt Pace and Billy Ray Halton standing in front of the bar, their faces a livid red. The short and stocky Halton was wearing a Navy Colt sitting low on his hip and thonged to his thigh. Pace, a thin, wiry man who wore a pair of guns, was jabbing the air with his finger as he traded insults with the younger man. Half a dozen patrons stood around watching intently, while the bartender waited nervously behind the bar.

"You're just a damned chicken-livered coward, Halton!" Pace shouted. "Why don't you just shut your stinkin' trap and meet me in the street where we can settle this once and for all?"

"I'll show you who's a coward!" raged Halton. "We can't get outta here fast enough for me! I'll put a bullet right—"

"*Billy Ray!*" Colby Tucker's voice thundered across the room.

Halton and Pace both turned to look at the sheriff. The saloon was suddenly blanketed in silence. Walt Stinn stood at the door as Tucker strode rigidly to the two men. "Billy Ray, you back off," the sheriff warned authoritatively.

Before Halton could respond, the tall lawman set his ice-blue eyes on the gunfighter and growled, "The last time we talked, Pace, I told you never to show up in Waco again. Your kind is not welcome here. Now, get out of my town!"

Curt Pace's craggy face grew redder and his jaw clenched. Turning to the bar, he picked up a half-empty shot glass, saying defiantly, "I'm not leavin' till my glass is empty."

Crossing to the bar in one long stride, Colby snatched the glass from Pace's bony hand and methodically poured the whiskey onto the floor. "Now it's empty," the lawman announced coldly, slamming the glass on the bar with a loud thump. "Your horse is waiting."

Billy Ray Halton finally found his voice and argued, "Now look, Sheriff. You've got no right—"

"Shut up, you pinheaded fool!" Colby blared at the young man while keeping his gaze steady on Pace's face. "You should be thanking me instead of arguing.

I'm trying to keep you from getting killed!" Then he snapped at Pace, "I said ride, mister."

There was fire in Curt Pace's eyes, and Colby Tucker could see the gunfighter's fingers twitching, his first instinct clearly being to draw on the sheriff. But Pace checked himself, apparently remembering Colby Tucker's reputation with a gun. Even though the lawman was more than twice Pace's age, the gunfighter did not choose to challenge him. Too many men who had tried it were now lying six feet deep in the ground.

Straightening his back and raising himself to full height, Pace stared unwaveringly at Colby for a few seconds, then turned and headed toward the door. He had just grabbed the edges of the batwings when Billy Ray Halton's words stopped him in his tracks.

"I guess now we all know who the coward is here, don't we, Pace?"

The gunslinger pivoted and his face was filled with fury. "Come on out in the street, Halton!" he roared. "I've got a bullet with your name on it that's just screamin' to taste your blood!"

The atmosphere in the saloon was thick with the two men's rage. Thrusting a finger in front of Halton's face, Colby rasped, "You shut up, Billy!" Then swinging the finger at Pace, he bellowed, "And I told *you* to ride! I won't say it again!"

Angrily pushing through the doors, Pace let the batwings swing wildly behind him as he stomped out of the saloon.

When he was out of sight, some of the patrons in the saloon commented on Colby's fearlessness in handling the famous gunslinger, and the lawman accepted their praise with a wry smile. Although he would not admit it publicly, he knew that his draw had slowed, and he wondered whether he could have taken Pace if there had been a shoot-out.

To break the tension in the saloon the bartender said

loudly, "Drinks for everyone on the house, fellas! Belly up to the bar." Smiling at the sheriff, he added, "Colby, I know you never touch liquor, but I've got some strong coffee brewin' back in the kitchen. Come on up here with the boys, and I'll get you some."

"Sounds good, Frank," the sheriff admitted, grinning. "Bring on the coffee."

Glancing arrogantly at the others, Billy Ray Halton tugged his hat brim down tight and headed for the door, stepping out into the brilliant sunlight. He stooped under the hitch rail and was about to untie his horse's reins when he heard his name barked from behind him in the middle of the street.

"Billy Ray," Curt Pace challenged, "you-gonna face me?"

Halton whirled about. The gunslinger's menacing figure, poised and ready to draw, was standing in the middle of the sun-bleached street. As people on the boardwalk stood and watched, young Halton stepped into the middle of the street. "You bet I'll face you," he answered stiffly.

Pace's hands were splayed over the butts of his revolvers, ready for action, while Halton, who for all his bragging had never actually drawn against a man, took his stance.

Mocking the younger man, Pace ordered, "Go to it, Halton!"

Billy Ray's hand started downward. Pace waited until the young tough's gun was on its way out of the holster, and then he drew his two revolvers with lightning speed. Before Halton could even level his muzzle, the impact of two .45 slugs slamming into his chest at the same instant lifted him off his feet, then dropped him flat on his back. His unfired gun lay in the dust by his motionless hand. He was dead.

Colby Tucker dashed out of the Lone Star and barreled toward the gunslinger, his face bespeaking his fury. The lawman did not get a chance to utter a word, however, before Curt Pace dropped his guns into their holsters and declared, "He drew first, Tucker. Just ask any of these folks here."

"He's telling the truth, Sheriff," called out one of Waco's leading citizens. "Billy Ray went for his gun first."

Running his gaze over the faces of the other witnesses, Colby Tucker found that they all concurred: Young Halton had drawn first. The sheriff glared at Pace. Narrowing his eyes, his voice hard and implacable, Colby told him, "This wouldn't have happened if you'd ridden out of here like I told you to. Billy Ray was just a kid, and you the same as murdered him."

"Now look, Tucker," Pace replied, raising his palms in protest, "that *kid*, as you call him, went for his gun, and I was just defending myself."

Glowering at the gunfighter, the lawman spat, "I can't arrest you for murder, Pace, but I *can* arrest you for disturbing the peace. And unfortunately for you, the circuit judge won't be back for another month—which means that you're going to stay locked in a jail cell until he hears your case." Colby's eyes grew even colder as he warned, "And if you resist arrest, I'll see that six months is added to your sentence. Now, drop your gun belt nice and easy."

Pace just stood there, his face reddening with fury.

Colby Tucker repeated his order. "I said drop your gun belt, Pace! *Now!*"

"There's no way I'm gonna stare through iron bars for a month," the gunslick declared.

Throwing caution aside, he went for both guns. As he did so, the sheriff's reflexes sprang to life, and his right hand was a blur as his gun came out of its holster. Three shots rang out.

Like an angry bee, one bullet plucked at Colby's left

sleeve, and another passed dangerously close to his right ear. Thirty feet away, the gunslinger staggered backward and fell. Half-dazed, the sheriff walked toward the fallen man and stood over him, seeing that the slug from his revolver had drilled Pace's heart. Life had already left the gunfighter.

Colby looked down at the rip in the sleeve where the bullet had barely missed him. Holstering his gun with a shaky hand, he looked around at the crowd and said, "Somebody get the undertaker."

As he turned and headed for his office several of the bystanders commented to him that his draw was as fast as it had ever been. Colby merely nodded and smiled, but he knew that what the people thought they saw was not really there. Curt Pace almost got him—and no man had ever come that close before. Wiping cold sweat from his brow, the silver-haired lawman told himself it was indeed time to take off the badge and hang up his gun.

Chapter Three

Morning came in a heavy, cloud-laden sky with a brisk wind whipping across the Texas hills, and as Colby Tucker rode into Waco right after breakfast, he cursed the wind and the dust it was blowing, for he had hoped it would be a nice day for Jim's induction as sheriff. Riding along Main Street toward his office, he peered through the swirling dust and recognized a young man named Elmer Simpson, the local sign painter, waiting for him on the boardwalk. Simpson was there to paint out Colby's name on the sign in front of the office and replace it with Jim's.

Bending his head against the wind and holding tight to his hat, Simpson greeted the sheriff as he dismounted. Colby squinted against the dust assailing his eyes and said, "Morning, Elmer." He shook his head and added, "Well, I guess the sign'll have to wait, since the dust would ruin your work for sure."

"Yeah, it's too bad about the wind, Sheriff, 'cause I know you wanted to surprise Jim by having his name already on the sign when he took office today. But you're right: Any flying dust would ruin the fresh paint. I'll just have to do it when the weather clears up." He bent down and picked up his paint and brushes. Turning to leave, he smiled at the lawman, telling him, "Well, I'll see you at the ceremony at ten. Sure hope the wind'll die down before then—and that those clouds behave themselves. Looks like we may get some rain before too long."

"I sure hope not," replied the lawman. "I'd like everything to be just right for Jim's sake."

Colby started to unlock his office when he noticed Waco's mayor, William Teague, and banker Morton Finney approaching from the other side of the street, clutching their hats.

"Morning, gents," Colby greeted them amiably. "Looks like we'll have to contend with the elements today."

"Indeed we will," Teague affirmed. Then he asked, "Could we see you for a minute or two, Colby?"

"Sure. Come on in."

Opening the door, Colby allowed the men to enter ahead of him, then stepped inside and closed the door. Gesturing toward a couple of chairs, he invited Teague and Finney to sit down.

"We really don't have time to sit and talk, Colby," the mayor explained, "but Mort and I just wanted to stop by and express our thanks to you for twenty-three years of excellent and faithful service. You've done the county proud, and we want you to know that we appreciate the kind of sheriff you've been all this time."

A lump formed in Colby Tucker's throat. Struggling for a moment against his emotions, he finally replied, "Gentlemen, I appreciate your telling me that. I've done my best to uphold the law in McLennan County, and I hope the rest of the people feel as you do about the way I've performed my duties."

Both men shook hands with Colby, saying they would see him at the ceremony, then left to buck the wind. The aging lawman stared after them for a moment, then took off his hat and sat down behind the desk. Suddenly it hit him that the office would no longer be his after ten o'clock that morning, and a strange ache settled in his breast. Letting his gaze roam around the room, he felt a touch of sadness wash over him. That his own son was going to have the job made it easier for him to accept the fact that this was his last day as sheriff, but still there was anguish in Colby Tucker's heart. A man didn't invest twenty-three years of his life in a place and then leave it all without some emotion.

The lawman decided he would not clean out all his personal things that day. Since Jim would be taking over, he would do it a little at a time. It would be easier that way.

His mind ran to Edie and how she had taken the news of his shoot-out with Curt Pace the day before, turning white when she saw how close the bullet had come when it ripped through his shirtsleeve. For her sake he was glad his lawman's career had come to an end, since in a lot of ways it truly had been a nightmare for her. But she was a trouper. Not once had she ever put pressure on him to quit. *Nope*, he thought wryly to himself, *good old Father Time has brought that about*.

Glancing up at the clock, Colby saw that it was nine-thirty. His heart started beating faster in anticipation of the imminent ceremony, and he decided that it would do him no good to sit in the office any longer. Standing up, he pulled on his hat, then headed toward the door. When he stepped outside, he was pleased to see that the wind had died down, but the clouds overhead remained dark and ominous. Rain was coming for sure. Colby Tucker locked the door behind him and started up the street toward the courthouse, where he would meet Edie, Jeff, and Jim and his family.

Reaching the courthouse square, the sheriff watched the banners and colorful decorations attached to the platform dancing in the slight breeze. A large crowd was gathering, which pleased him. Apparently people from all over McLennan County were coming to say farewell to him and to give Jim a big welcome as sheriff. A lawman had it tough enough butting heads with all the outlaws and riffraff that came down the pike. He most certainly needed to know that the people he protected were behind him.

He walked over to the courthouse, where his wife, two sons, daughter-in-law, and grandchildren were standing and chatting with William Teague. After a few minutes of small talk Sheriff Colby Tucker escorted his family onto the platform, and they all took their seats. At precisely ten o'clock Mayor Teague strode to the podium at the front of the platform, preparing to address the crowd.

Colby glanced at his wife, who sat to his right. There were mixed emotions written on Edie's face. She was obviously relieved to know that her husband would no longer be wearing a badge or a gun . . . but she felt the weight of knowing her older son would now carry the responsibility as sheriff of McLennan County. The badge on a sheriff's chest was always more of a target than that of his deputy.

The mayor gave a ten-minute speech in which he honored Colby Tucker for his years of service as sheriff of McLennan County. In his closing remarks Teague sprinkled in a few well-placed jokes about old age. Colby was touched deeply when the mayor presented him with a check in the amount of five hundred dollars on behalf of the county. All the county officials had secretly taken donations from the residents, their way of expressing gratitude for a job well done.

Comic relief was abruptly provided when a couple of Colby's gray-haired friends came running up, carrying a brand-new rocking chair. The crowd laughed and applauded as the chair was presented to the outgoing lawman as a retirement gift, and Colby protested with mock indignation that he would not be needing the chair for at least another twenty years.

As the laughter died down, Mayor William Teague then addressed the crowd again, telling them, "And now the time has come to install Jim Tucker officially as our new county sheriff. Jim's done a fine job as his father's deputy, and he won your vote to carry on the fine Tucker tradition. Turning to the younger Tucker, the mayor ordered, "Hand me your badge, Jim." When the former deputy removed his badge and handed it to Teague, the mayor then called for him to raise his right hand, and he swore him in as sheriff of McLennan County.

Colby Tucker rose to his feet and moved beside his son. With emotion choking him, the aging, handsome man removed the badge from his own chest, then looked his son in the eye. Speaking loudly enough for the crowd to hear his words, he said, "Jim, I'm mighty proud to have you wear the badge that I have worn for so many years. I know you'll make the people of McLennan County glad they put you in office."

With trembling hands the former lawman pinned the badge on his elder son, then embraced him while he fought back tears. The crowd broke into applause and gave both men a rousing ovation. The ovation subsided when thunder rumbled overhead and rain began to splatter, scattering the crowd.

A jagged bolt of lightning split the dark sky, and the Tucker family all headed for shelter as well. They gathered under the porch of the dry goods store as thunder boomed.

Jeff walked over to his older brother and clapped him on the shoulder. "Jim, I know you'll make us all proud of you." Then, buttoning up the slicker he had worn, the young marshal announced that he had to head back immediately to Nacogdoches.

"You have to go off now? In this weather?" his mother asked, concern in her voice.

"I'm afraid so, Ma." He grinned at her. "I'll be fine, I promise." He kissed her cheek, embraced his father and brother, then kissed Nelda and the two children.

"Congratulations," he told Jim once again, and then he leaped off the porch and ran for his horse.

The family watched him ride away in the driving rain.

Jim put his arm around his wife's shoulders. Smiling proudly at her and his children, he asked, "What do you say we all go to the new sheriff's office?"

Raising his voice above the cracking of the thunder and lightning, Colby told his son, "I've still got some of my things at the office, but I'll pick them up later. It's all yours now." Clapping his son on the shoulder, he added, "I've also still got my name on the office sign. I was going to surprise you by having your name painted on it earlier, but the wind was stirring up so much dust, Elmer Simpson has to wait till the weather clears."

Jim patted his father's back and said, "Thanks, Dad. I appreciate your thinking of it. But remember, this office will always be yours, in a way, 'cause you've left your mark on it. And I want you to feel free to come by anytime you want."

"If you don't mind, Jim, I'm going to do my darndest to see that he doesn't," Edie Tucker wryly told her son as she hugged him. Then, taking her husband's arm and holding a large umbrella over their heads, she led the former lawman to their carriage, which fortunately had the top up. While Edie settled herself on the seat, Colby tied his horse to the back. Climbing in beside his wife, the former sheriff clucked to the horse, and they drove through the downpour to their ranch.

When the Tuckers arrived home, Colby let Edie out of the carriage at the back porch, then drove through the rain to the barn. He entered the house a few minutes later, dripping wet, and Edie approached him, holding a towel for his hair, and suggested, "You better get into some dry clothes before you catch your death."

Removing his hat and hanging it on a peg next to the

kitchen door, the tall man took the towel from her hand and ran it over his wet hair, answering, "I will as soon as I do something that I know will make you very happy."

Edie looked at him curiously as he tossed the towel onto a chair and headed out of the kitchen, but she held her tongue.

Walking through the parlor of the two-story house, he mounted the stairs. When he reached the second floor, he ambled down a long hallway, then climbed another staircase and pushed open a squeaky door. Entering the attic, he could hear the hard rain beating on the roof. In the dim light that came through two small windows, he made his way to a large trunk and lifted the lid. Then he unbuckled his gun belt and wrapped the belt around the gun and holster, placing it reverently inside the trunk. Before dropping the lid, he stared at the gun belt for a long moment, then sighed. He eased the lid down slowly and left the attic.

Edie was waiting for him in the parlor when he reached the bottom of the staircase. She noticed the absence of the gun belt, and a relieved smile worked its way across her lovely face. "Thank goodness," she declared. "You'll never have to wear that awful thing again."

Feeling a mixture of relief and sadness, Colby Tucker took his wife in his arms and held her.

Lightning slashed the dark gray sky, turning the world around Duke Malone and his two cohorts a glaring white as they hunched against the driving rain.

"We'll be nearin' Waco in about an hour," Mad Dog Malone shouted above the downpour, "and I've got my plan all worked out. The jury foreman, Horace Deming —he lives a couple of miles south of town, so we'll head there first. Then my unfaithful ex-wife is gonna die . . . her and that wife-stealin' new husband of hers. Once they're dead, we'll go on into town and I'll send Sheriff Colby Tucker to meet his maker."

"We'd better be careful about being seen," Harry Blevins put in. "We sure don't need any local law on our tails."

"The only local law is the sheriff," replied Malone, "and since he's gonna die real soon, we ain't got much to worry about."

"Is your wife still living at your old house?" queried George Niles.

The killer's eyes narrowed angrily. "Nope. They're livin' at Ted Daly's spread. He was our neighbor—his place was just a mile down the road from ours." Pausing, Malone added bitterly, "Mighty convenient, wouldn't you say?"

Neither of the ex-guards answered.

"Anyway," Malone continued, "after I've taken care of those four, we'll head for the Red River. We'll dig up the money, and then we'll track down Hans Brummer. He's the one who turned me in to Colby Tucker. Once we find Brummer and I have the sweet pleasure of killin' him nice and slow, we'll gather a few more men and go on a robbin' spree."

"Let's not forget to keep an eye on our back trail," put in Niles. "There'll be federal marshals after us, sure as anything."

"Right," agreed Malone. "We'll probably have to kill us some of those government men."

"I was just thinking," Blevins muttered, "is there any chance that money won't still be there? I mean, weren't there some other gang members who knew where you buried it?"

Malone shook his head and replied, "Just one: a fella named Dick Blair. He and I pulled off that heist together. Not long after we buried it, we had a shoot-out with a town marshal and two of his deputies—and Dick took a slug in the battle. I killed the three lawmen, but

Dick died before I could get him to a doctor . . . so I'm the only man alive who knows where the money is buried. I can guarantee you, it's still there—safe, sound, and dry."

The trio fell silent as they continued through the slanting, wind-driven rain. Finally Duke Malone led them to a thick stand of willows and reined in, pointing through the trees to a large, stately house thirty yards away.

"That's Deming's place," the killer growled. "He lives mighty high on the hog, don't he?"

Swinging from his saddle, Malone tied his horse to a branch and said to his partners, "You boys wait here. I'll go take my pleasure and be back in a few minutes."

Dashing through the trees, the killer ran through the Deming yard and stealthily eased up onto the back porch. He removed his hat and shook the water from it, then pulled his right-hand gun. He pounded on the door with his left fist, waited a few seconds, then pounded again. When there was no response, he swore, raised a foot, and battered the door. It swung open, slamming against the wall inside.

Malone charged in, finding himself in a large pantry behind the kitchen. Just as he was about to move through the kitchen toward the front of the house, a small, elderly woman appeared. She had a cane in her hand, and she raised it as if to defend herself.

"Who are you, and what do you want?" she demanded.

Ignoring her questions, Malone strode up to her and said icily, "I remember you. You're Lucille Deming. I saw you in the courthouse every day, lookin' superior. Where's your husband?"

"You've ruined my door!" Lucille cried. "What are you doing in my house?"

"I want to see your husband," Malone replied coldly.

Waving her cane at him, she screamed, "Get out of here! Do you hear me? I said get out of here!"

With his free hand the killer seized the cane and wrenched it from her grasp. Her eyes bulged with fear, and she backed up, obviously terrified that he was going to strike her with the cane. Instead he threw it across the kitchen and pushed past the old woman, knocking her down. He waved the gun around as he hurried through the house, entering room after room. Finally, after thoroughly searching every room and finding no one else in the house, Malone holstered his gun as he angrily returned to the kitchen.

Lucille Deming had inched her way to a wall and was sitting against it, her face a mixture of fear and anger. Malone strode over to where she sat and, looming over her, glared furiously. Through clenched teeth he commanded, "I'm gonna ask you one more time, old woman. Where's your husband? Is he at your store?"

Lucille Deming eyed him steadily, then exclaimed, "I . . . I know who you are! You're that killer! The one they call Mad Dog! How did you get out of prison? You were sentenced to life!"

"I walked out, dearie," Duke replied drily. Then his voice grew colder. "When do you expect your old man to get home?"

Lucille's lower lip trembled. "Horace is never coming home," she said shakily. "He's dead."

"*Dead?*" Leaning over, Duke jerked the elderly woman up by one arm and growled, "What do you mean he's dead?"

Gasping, she winced. "You're hurting me."

Keeping the pressure on her arm, Malone insisted, "You're makin' up that story so I don't find him and kill him, ain't you? Horace ain't dead!"

Tears glistened in the elderly woman's eyes as she replied, "I'm not making anything up. He died eighteen months ago. Of heart failure."

Malone's temper rose. Shaking her hard, he snarled, "You're lyin'! Nobody's gonna cheat me outta killin' that dirty skunk! He did his best to get the judge to hang me, now it's only right that I get my revenge! You better tell me the truth, or I'll break your arm!"

"I *am* telling you the truth," she whimpered. "I can prove it to you."

"Oh, yeah? Then hop to it!"

He let go of her arm and followed her as she hobbled into a small room off the main hallway. From the top drawer of a rolltop desk, she pulled out an old scrapbook. Resting the book on the sliding cover of the desk, she opened it and removed a newspaper clipping. Handing it to Malone, she told him, "There. Read it for yourself. That is, if you *can* read."

Sneering at her, Malone grabbed the clipping and walked through the dim room to a window. Holding it toward the light, he slowly read the clipping from the *Waco Herald,* an obituary reporting Horace Deming's departure from this life on October 12, 1878. He had indeed died of heart failure.

Duke Malone's face purpled with unbridled rage. "No!" he screeched. "That ain't fair! I got a right to kill him!"

The elderly woman looked into his cold eyes and shook her head. "You're too late for that, Mr. Malone. Now, would you please leave my house—and leave me alone."

Malone's temples throbbed and his breathing was erratic. "Sorry, old woman, but I can't do that. You can identify me . . . and that won't do at all. Nope, I'm afraid you're gonna have to die," he spat.

Her face blanched, and Lucille Deming began pleading with the killer to spare her. "I promise I won't tell a soul you've been here," she cried. But without warning Duke Malone grabbed her and clamped his hands around her neck, squeezing her windpipe with his thumbs. She valiantly fought him, but she was too small and too weak. The life left her quickly.

The killer let her body fall to the floor, then stood over her, thinking about how to dispose of the body. He remembered seeing a well house in the backyard; if the shaft was wide enough, he could dump Lucille Deming down the well. Picking the woman up and slinging her over his shoulder, Mad Dog Malone carried her out the back door.

As he walked across the yard Malone looked through the trees and saw Harry Blevins and George Niles waiting on the other side of the grove of willows. He could tell by their expressions that they were surprised to see the woman over his shoulder, her head and hands dangling lifelessly. The killer then entered the well house, dumped his burden down the well, and reappeared outside within moments.

When Duke Malone walked over to his partners, sitting on their horses, Blevins stared at him, his face registering shock. "You killed that old woman?"

"Yep, she was Deming's wife," Malone replied as he untied his horse from a small tree.

"But why?"

" 'Cause she could tell the law I was here."

"But surely there could've been another way. And what about her husband?"

"Deming's dead. Has been for a year and a half. So killin' his wife's as close as I could get to killin' him," Malone told him defensively.

"Yeah, but an old woman . . ." complained Niles. "Duke, you shouldn't—"

"I'll kill who I want to kill, George!" snapped Malone as he settled into his saddle. "Don't you try to become my conscience—leastways, not if you plan on gettin' your share of that fifty thousand dollars."

"Okay, okay," Niles responded in a placating voice. "I just—"

"Better let it go, George," spoke up Blevins. "Let's just get out of here."

*   *   *

By the time the three men rode into the yard of the Daly ranch three quarters of an hour later, the rain had abated somewhat. As they approached the house Malone commanded, "You guys wait out here. If anybody comes runnin' out, tryin' to get away, stop 'em." He noticed the two men eyeing each other furtively and growled, "Let me tell you somethin'. Bein' in my gang means doin' your share—and if that share means killin' somebody when necessary, then you'll do it! Understood?"

Blevins and Niles looked glumly at each other, and after a brief pause Blevins answered, "Sure, Duke."

Slipping from his saddle, Malone walked around the house and outbuildings, looking for his ex-wife and her new husband. There were horses and cattle in the corral by the barn, but there were no people in sight. He headed for the house, halting short of the first step when the door opened and a man appeared. The killer's hands dropped for his guns, but he checked himself when he realized the man was clearly not Ted Daly. Glancing to the man's right, Malone could see three children at a window and a woman who was not Marian.

Smiling tentatively, the man said, "Howdy, stranger. What are you doing out on a day like this?"

Malone stepped up on the porch to get out of the cold drizzle. Removing his hat and shaking the water from it, he said, "I'm lookin' for Marian and Ted Daly. Looks like they don't live here no more."

"No, sir," responded the rancher. "We bought the place from the Dalys four years ago. They moved up north. Bought a ranch somewhere near Fort Worth."

Setting his cold black eyes on the man, Malone asked, "You know any more than that? I mean, like *whereabouts* near Fort Worth?"

"Nope, sorry, I'm afraid that's all I know. They told

us that much when we bought the place from them, and we haven't seen or heard from them since."

Malone merely nodded curtly and walked away. Frustrated for the second time that day, the killer wordlessly mounted his horse, spurring it savagely, and headed toward Waco, his two cohorts following him.

As Duke Malone, Harry Blevins, and George Niles rode into town, there was hardly anyone out on the streets of Waco. Apparently the rain, falling harder now, had driven them all indoors. From time to time someone darted from one shop to another, but no one crossed the street, which was a sea of mud. The wind had picked up again along with the rain, whipping spray relentlessly into the three men's faces as they headed toward the sheriff's office.

A middle-aged couple dashed from the general store toward the dress shop, and the man flicked a glance at the riders. Inside the shop Henry Bottoms looked at his wife and gasped, "Sadie, did you recognize him?"

"Who, Henry?" Sadie Bottoms responded somewhat impatiently.

"The man on that horse out there! It was Duke Malone . . . Mad Dog Malone!"

The heads of others in the shop turned at the familiar name. Sadie started toward the door to open it and take a look for herself, but her husband jumped in front of her.

"No! Don't open the door! I don't want him to know we've seen him!"

Putting her hands on her hips, Sadie gave her husband an irritated look and said, "You've got to be mistaken, Henry. Duke Malone is in prison for the rest of his life. Don't you remember?"

Shaking his head, Bottoms said, "I know he's *supposed* to be, dear . . . but that's him out there. I know it is."

*   *   *

Sitting on his horse across from the sheriff's office, Duke Malone peered through the rain at the sign nailed to the left of the office door. The town had changed dramatically since he had been in prison, and he wanted to make sure Colby Tucker was still sheriff. He came close to smiling when, squinting, he was able to read the lettering on the sign:

McLennan County Sheriff's Office
Colby Tucker, Sheriff

Malone nodded to each of his partners, then stared across at the sheriff's office again, determining just the right moment to make his move. Suddenly the door opened and a small man wearing what looked like a Western Union cap hurried out the door and up the street.

Malone waited until the man had disappeared from sight. Then, inching his horse a little farther across the street, he strained to see through the rain-splattered window. Inside the office a lamp shone onto the desk, and Malone could make out the form of a tall, broad-shouldered man seated behind the desk, apparently engrossed in his work.

Malone pulled the stolen Winchester rifle from the saddleboot, then dismounted and stepped into the mud, motioning for Blevins to take his reins. The killer walked slowly across the street, glancing around with each step. Lining himself up squarely with the window, he watched the man behind the desk. Although his face was obscured by the rain on the glass, his outline was clear enough. Malone could even make out the badge on his chest, shining brightly in the lamplight.

Carefully scanning the street, Malone saw no one. Satisfaction washed over him as he levered a cartridge into the chamber and shouldered the rifle, for thirty feet away sat the man who had arrested him and sent him to prison . . . and now Sheriff Colby Tucker was going to die.

Malone sighted down the wet barrel, drawing a bead on the glint of the badge, and squeezed the trigger. The Winchester roared, glass shattered, and McLennan County's sheriff was blasted backward off his chair.

Racing back across the street through the mud and leaping onto his horse, Duke Malone and his partners sped out of town. Just before they turned a corner, the killer looked back over his shoulder, seeing people rushing out of the shops lining Main Street and hurrying toward the sheriff's office. Malone almost smiled for the second time that day. One down, three to go. Taking out Colby Tucker more than made up for his disappointment at losing the chance to murder Horace Deming—and having to search for his unfaithful wife and her husband before he got his revenge on them. Still, he would eventually find them. And when he did . . .

Chapter Four

Glancing out the kitchen window as he worked on a cupboard door that Edie had asked him to repair, Colby Tucker noticed that the sky was beginning to grow lighter. It seemed that at last the rain had all but stopped.

Colby was just about to reset some hinges when he heard a knock on the front door of the house. He paused and put down his tools, preparing to answer the knock, when Edie called from the end of the hallway, saying that she would get the door. Colby Tucker smiled to himself. His wife was not about to let even the smallest interruption interfere with his task, one of several odd jobs that had needed tending to for months.

Edie came into the kitchen, followed by Don Graham, a rough-hewn man in his late fifties who was one of Colby's best friends. "Don says he has something to tell us, Colby," Edie said uneasily.

One look at Graham's deathly pale face told the former lawman that something was very wrong. Laying down his screwdriver, Colby declared, "Don, you look like you've seen a ghost. What's happened? Have you had some trouble at the gun shop? If you have, that's Jim's business now, not mine."

Graham took off his hat and ran a trembling hand through his thinning hair. Licking his lips nervously, he flicked his eyes between Colby and Edie and said,

"Colby . . . Edie . . . I . . . I've got some real bad news. I'm not sure how to tell you this."

Walking to his friend, Colby asked firmly, "What is it, Don?"

Graham seemed unable to answer. Laying his hand on Colby's arm, he finally mumbled, "Maybe . . . maybe you and Edie should sit down."

Colby looked his friend square in the eyes and demanded, "Tell me, Don, what's wrong?"

A tear started down Don Graham's left cheek. "It's Jim. He's . . . he's dead."

Colby's mouth sagged and Edie fell heavily onto a kitchen chair. The former sheriff immediately stepped to his wife and put a comforting hand on her shoulder. Looking at Don Graham, he gasped, "How? . . . What happened? We just left there!"

"It . . . it happened shortly after Jim began working. Somebody shot him through the office window, Colby. A few people saw three men gallop north out of town just after the rifle was fired. Edie, Colby, I'm so sorry . . . I'd have brought Reverend Harris along to be with you, but he's out of town till later today."

Edie Tucker began to weep, holding her hands to her face. The full impact of Jim's death suddenly hit Colby like a battering ram in the chest. His knees turned to water, and he felt as though there were a steel band around his chest.

His old friend grabbed a chair and pulled it next to Edie's, then he took Colby by the arm and helped him sit down. Hot tears spilled down Colby's face as he struggled to find his voice. Above Edie's crying he murmured, "Hang on, darlin'. I'm with you."

Don Graham stood beside them, twisting his hat in his hands. "God, I wish there was something I could do for you. I feel so helpless."

His voice choking, Colby responded, "Thanks, Don.

We appreciate your concern. But there's nothing you can do to ease the pain."

Suddenly the grief-stricken Edie Tucker turned and flung her arms around her husband, sobbing uncontrollably, and Colby wept with her.

After a few minutes the Tuckers' crying subsided. Keeping a comforting hand on his wife's arm, Colby asked his friend, "The people who saw the three men ride away . . . did they recognize any of them?"

"Not so far as I know," replied Graham. "It all happened so fast, and everybody was indoors, keeping out of the rain. When they heard the shot, they looked out, but the killers were already galloping away. Besides, it was raining so hard that someone would've had a hard time recognizing his own brother at that moment."

Tears began coursing down Colby's face again as he asked, "Tell me . . . is . . . is anybody with the . . . body?"

"Bill Teague is there, Colby. He said to tell you he won't let anybody into the office until you get there. He knows you'll want to find someone to come stay with Edie before you leave here, and he'll wait as long as is necessary."

Grabbing a kitchen towel to use as a handkerchief, Edie Tucker dried her teary face and blew her nose. "I'll . . . I'll be all right by myself, dear," she told her husband in a quivering voice. Then she gasped and asked Graham, "Don! Nelda and the children—has anyone told them what's happened?"

"No," Don Graham replied, shaking his head sadly. "Bill and I discussed it, and we thought it best to let you and Colby decide how to handle that. Certainly they should be told as soon as possible."

Biting her lip, Edie drew a shaky breath and looked tearfully at her husband. "It should be you and me to tell them, Colby."

The silver-haired man gazed tenderly at his wife and
offered, "Maybe it'd be best if I got one of the neighbors to stay with you, honey. I can break it to Nelda
and the kids."

Shaking her head firmly, Edie insisted, "I would
rather be there when they hear it. Nelda will need
me."

Thinking it through, Colby decided Edie was right.
After sending Don Graham back to town to inform
Mayor Teague that he would be there shortly, Colby
pulled on his jacket and went out to the barn to hitch
the horse to the carriage. When he came back into the
house a few minutes later, Colby found that Edie was
ready to go. With his arm around her he escorted her
out to the carriage and helped her in, and they headed
into town. Looking up at the sky, Colby Tucker thought
how ironic it was that the storm clouds were finally
breaking up overhead—yet in their hearts, they were
just settling in.

Nelda Tucker did indeed need Edie's strength and
support when she was given the terrible news of her
husband's murder. Colby stayed with his daughter-in-
law and grandchildren for over an hour, doing all he
could to comfort them; then, leaving Edie with them,
he drove the carriage to the sheriff's office.

There was a small crowd gathered in front of the
office, and Waco's undertaker, Paul Yelland, was among
the bystanders. As Colby alighted from the carriage and
approached the office, everyone in the crowd expressed
their sympathy.

Yelland detached himself from the others and hurried
to meet Colby. "Please know that my heart goes out to
you," the undertaker said softly.

Fighting back his tears, the former lawman replied,
"Thanks, Paul. I appreciate that." He paused a moment, then asked, "Have you taken Jim away yet?"

"No, I haven't. Bill Teague is inside with Don Graham, and they didn't want anyone in there disturbing anything until you had come."

Laying a hand on Yelland's shoulder, Colby told him, "You wait out here, Paul. I'll call for you when I'm ready."

Don Graham had apparently been watching for Colby's arrival, for as soon as Colby's muddy boots touched the boardwalk, the office door opened and Graham ushered him inside. The murmurs of the crowd outside abruptly ceased when Graham closed the door behind him, and the room was utterly silent. Removing his hat, Colby looked over at William Teague, who stood in front of the desk, his face a mask of sorrow.

"Colby, I feel terrible about this," the mayor said softly, his voice breaking.

"Thanks, Bill," the ex-sheriff responded, nodding. Sighing deeply, he asked, "Where is he?"

"I . . . I would have put his body in a different position and covered it," Teague told him apologetically, "but I thought it best not to touch anything until you got here." Gesturing behind the desk with a shaky hand, Teague said, "He's right back here."

Colby laid his hat on a chair, wiped a hand across his mustache, and circled around the desk, feeling a cold, hollow dread. He had seen many a dead man, but he was not prepared to look upon the lifeless body of his own son. Steeling himself, he looked down. Jim Tucker lay on his back with his legs hooked over the seat of the overturned chair. His eyes were closed—for which Colby was thankful—but his mouth sagged open.

Breathing raggedly, the stricken father knelt down beside his dead son. When he saw the bullet hole dead-centered through the badge, he first whimpered, then moaned. There was very little blood on Jim's vest and shirt. His boy had died instantly.

Both grief and wrath boiled up inside Colby Tucker, and he closed his eyes and gritted his teeth, fighting to keep his composure. His whole body shook, and he wanted to release a wild, primal scream, but he suppressed it. Feeling Don Graham's consoling hand on his shoulder, a calmness came over him, and the maelstrom within him began to subside. When he had gained control of his emotions, he turned his head and spoke over his shoulder.

"Don . . . Bill . . . who could have done this? *Why* did they do it?"

"Maybe you should look at this, Colby," suggested Teague.

Colby Tucker rose to his feet and looked through tear-dimmed eyes at the piece of paper in the mayor's hand. It was a Western Union telegram. As Teague handed it to the ex-sheriff, he said, "After I found this telegram on Jim's desk, I talked to Charlie Melton. He told me he had brought this to Jim no more than five minutes before the shot was fired."

The former lawman noted that the wire was addressed to him. Scanning it quickly, Colby felt his scalp tighten as he read of the murder of Texas State Prison Warden Neal Alton and the subsequent flight of Duke Malone. The killer was believed to be heading north with two former guards, Harry Blevins and George Niles, who had helped him to escape. The telegram had been sent by the acting warden of the Huntsville facility, who felt that Colby should know about the breakout since he had learned—through interrogating prisoners—that Malone had been bragging he would escape and kill the man who had put him in prison, along with all the other people he felt had done him wrong.

When he had finished reading, Colby Tucker stood silently, rubbing his chin.

"Do you think what I do?" asked William Teague.

"That it was Malone who killed Jim?" Shaking his head, the mayor added, "What with the rain coming down as hard as it was then, probably Malone couldn't tell it was Jim he was shooting at, not you. You and Jim were exactly the same size, and your name's still on the sign out front. Seems to me Duke Malone killed your son—all the while thinking he was killing you."

There was an abrupt knock at the door, and Don Graham walked across the room and opened it. Recognizing the small man who stood there, he said curtly, "What is it, Henry? We're awfully busy right now."

"I need to talk to Colby," Henry Bottoms insisted, looking past the gun-shop owner to the ex-sheriff. "It's very important."

"Does it have to do with the present situation?" queried Graham.

"It sure does."

"Come in, Henry," spoke up Colby, his voice weary and sad.

When the door was closed, Bottoms said, "Colby, Sadie and I have been talking with folks on the street about this . . . shooting incident. I figured someone else had recognized Duke Malone, but apparently I'm the only one that got a clear look at him."

Colby's eyes widened. "You actually *saw* Duke Malone, Henry?"

"Yes, sir. It was him, all right. Sadie and I were going into the dress shop right across the street when Malone and two other fellows rode up. Stopped right in front of me, they did. When Malone turned to speak to the men he was with, his face was turned directly toward me. I pulled Sadie into the shop and closed the door. Didn't want him to see *us*." Henry Bottoms paused, then continued, "I thought since no one else seems to have gotten a good look at Malone, you'd want to know that it was definitely him, Colby."

"You're right, Henry, and I appreciate your telling me."

Backing toward the door, Bottoms offered just before exiting, "Sadie and I want you to know that you all have our condolences, Colby."

When the door closed behind Henry Bottoms, Colby Tucker swore angrily. Turning to Graham and Teague, he growled, "Well, I guess that clinches it. If there was any doubt that Duke Malone killed Jim, there sure isn't anymore." He stood silently fuming for a few minutes, then he asked Graham to get the undertaker.

Kneeling beside his dead son again, he tenderly removed the bullet-drilled badge from Jim's chest and held it in his palm, studying it for a long moment. When Don Graham and the undertaker came in, Colby put the badge in his shirt pocket.

"I brought the hearse, Colby," advised Yelland. "If you're ready for me to . . . uh . . . take Jim over to my place, I'll bring in the stretcher. My assistant is waiting outside, ready to help me."

Colby swallowed hard, then nodded. He turned his head away while his son's body was being removed.

When the sheet-draped body had been placed in the hearse, the undertaker returned to the office and said, "You want to talk about the funeral later, Colby?"

The former lawman sighed. "No. No sense putting it off, Paul." He was quiet for a few moments, then said, "Let's bury Jim tomorrow morning. That is, if you can do it and Reverend Harris will be available."

"No problem for me," replied Yelland. "I'll check with the preacher right away and let you know. He should be back by now. You advise me if Nelda wants it some other way."

Shaking his head, Colby responded, "I'm thinking of her *and* his mother. The quicker it's done and over with, the better it will be for them." He put on his hat and walked to the door, then turned to Don Graham and William Teague. "Thanks for your help. I'd better go send a telegram off to Jeff and let him know what's happened."

Graham put a comforting arm around Colby Tucker's shoulder as they walked toward the door, telling his old friend, "It's too bad Jeff won't be here for the funeral. I know his presence would mean a lot to you and Edie."

His hand on the doorknob, Colby paused and sighed. "It would indeed. Well, I figure I'll also wire the marshals in a couple of the towns that Jeff'll be passing through on his way to Nacogdoches, asking them to give him the news of Jim's murder if they should see him. Maybe this lousy weather's slowed him down some so he won't have gone too far and he'll be able to return to Waco and be with us soon."

The Texas sky was clear the next morning, and at ten o'clock, under a brilliant sun that was already drying up the muddy earth, a crowd was gathered around a gravesite in the Waco cemetery, attending the funeral of Sheriff Jim Tucker.

The coffin that held the young sheriff's body rested on taut ropes over the yawning hole in the ground, and the Tucker family, minus Jeff, stood nearest the coffin while the minister read from the Scriptures. Nelda and Edie, dressed entirely in black with thin veils shielding their faces, stood on either side of the tall, silver-haired Colby, drawing strength from him, while Sam and Susie Tucker hovered close to their mother.

Colby hardly heard the preacher's words of comfort to the family; instead, he was having a difficult time keeping the face of Duke Malone from preying on his mind.

The service was finally concluded, and after all their friends and neighbors had expressed their sorrow, the Tuckers prepared to leave. Nelda and her children were staying with Colby and Edie for a few days, and the two women were glad they had each other for comfort.

The family walked away from the gravesite and found Mayor William Teague and the four members of Waco's town council waiting by the cemetery gate to speak with Colby Tucker. Approaching the grieving father, his hat in his hand, Teague looked uncomfortable. "Colby, we need to talk to you."

Colby excused himself for a moment to Teague. Turning to Edie and Nelda, he put a hand on each of their shoulders and told them, "You take the buckboard and go on home with the kids. I'll be there shortly."

Sniffling slightly, Edie asked, "How will you get there?"

"We'll drive him, Edie," Teague spoke up. "And don't worry. We won't keep him long."

Colby watched the wagon drive off, then faced the mayor. "I assume you want me to wear the sheriff's badge again."

"I hate to ask for your help at a time like this, but as you realize, this county is without a sheriff—heck, we don't even have a deputy. You also know that the Waco council has the authority to appoint a man to the office in a case like this, and if you could take over, just until we can get a permanent replacement . . . We know you wanted to retire—and stay retired—but we've got to have a sheriff."

Colby was silent for a moment, then he stared hard at the mayor. "I'm going after Malone, Bill," he said flatly.

"But surely federal marshals are on his trail," Teague declared.

"No doubt," Colby agreed, nodding. "But Malone killed my son—and I'm the man who's gonna get him."

"You've never struck me as the vigilante type, Colby,"

the mayor remarked, arching his eyebrows. "I never thought you'd—"

"I'm not," Colby rejoined quickly. "I want you to swear me back in as sheriff, just as you wanted." Pulling the bullet-drilled badge out of his shirt pocket, he added, "I'll wear this badge, but you'll have to get a new deputy sheriff quick, because as lawman of McLennan County, I'm going after Duke Malone. If I can, I'll bring him in for trial—our new judge isn't like the one who refused to hang Malone six years ago, and this one'll hang him for sure—but if Mad Dog resists arrest, I'll kill him. Once he's dead—one way or the other—I'll resign again. I've given this some thought, and if you send a wire to Crawford, there's a good chance Marshal Lang will let you have his deputy, Wayne Dunne, to act as deputy here until a replacement can be found."

Teague was silent for a moment, then he asked cautiously, "Colby, don't you think it would be better to let the federal men handle Malone? I mean . . . you are really awfully involved here. Your judgment might not—"

"My judgment's just what it should be," Colby Tucker replied in a voice as cold as his ice-blue eyes. "That bastard thought he was killing *me* when he cut Jim down, Bill! That gives me more than the right to be the man to put a rope around his filthy neck! I promise you I'll do my best to bring him in for trial. But if he forces me to, I'll certainly put a bullet through that piece of steel he calls a heart."

The mayor looked at his four councilmen, and they all shrugged, apparently realizing they would get no further trying to talk the lawman into letting someone else take Duke Malone. Changing the subject slightly, Teague said, "Colby, do you think Jeff might be willing to take the sheriff's job on a permanent basis? Since he's a Tucker, I have no doubt the people of this county would give him the nod."

"You can ask him yourself when he gets here, Bill,"
answered Colby. "He's bound to arrive in Waco some-
time in the next few days. Meanwhile, I suggest you
swear me back in as sheriff."

Immediately after the swearing in, Colby Tucker was
driven home by Bill Teague. As he strode up the front
steps and into his house, Colby fingered his son's badge
in his pocket. He would not pin it back on until after he
rode off, fearing the sight of the bullet hole would be
too painful a reminder for Edie and Nelda of Jim's
terrible death. The aging sheriff felt a bit guilty at the
speed with which he offered his services as a lawman so
soon after promising Edie that his days of facing danger
were over. But his guilt was allayed at the thought that
his son's death demanded such an action; there was
simply no other choice to make.

Meeting her husband at the front door, Edie's face
fell when she read the look of determination on her
husband's face. "Oh, Colby!" she gasped. "You've told
the town council that you'll be sheriff again, haven't
you?"

"I know I've disappointed you, Edie. The last thing I
ever intended was to wear a badge again."

"Promise me it will just be for a short while, Colby. I
mean, the council will find someone else to take over
the job permanently, won't they?"

The sheriff sighed. "I suppose they will. But that's
not the reason I told them I'd fill in, Edie. I offered to
become sheriff again for the sole purpose of capturing
Duke Malone."

"Colby, no!" Edie shouted. "I've just lost my son! I
don't want to lose my husband, too! Why do you have
to be the one to go after him?"

The aging lawman took his wife's hands in his own
and softly told her, "That killer murdered our Jim, and

I've got to track him down. I wouldn't be able to live with myself if I wasn't the one who went after him. Please say you understand."

Sniffling, Edie looked deep into his eyes, then wordlessly nodded.

Colby gathered his wife in his arms, and they stood embracing for a long moment. Finally she pulled away from him and asked, "Do you know where you're going to start looking for Malone?"

"According to the warden at the Texas State Prison, Malone had done some bragging about getting even with the people who put him away—people he swore to kill when he escaped." His voice choked up when he added, "No doubt my name was at the top of his list—which is why Jim was shot. My guess is he's also planning to murder his former partner, Hans Brummer, since Brummer turned state's evidence, and probably also his ex-wife, Marian Daly, since she didn't stand by him. Seems I remember Marian and Ted moved somewhere up north when they left here three or four years ago. Think I'll ride out to the ranch where they used to live and see if the folks who bought the place have any idea where the Dalys are living now. I've got to do my best to catch Malone before he finds them."

Moments later Colby went up to the attic, taking his gun belt, holster, and gun from the trunk where he had so recently packed them. When he came back downstairs and Edie saw him with the gun belt on, she began to weep.

Colby took Edie in his arms and held her tight. "Darlin'," he said softly, "I was so hoping I would never have to wear this again. And I'll make you a solemn vow that once this is over, this gun'll go back into the attic—and this time it'll stay there for good."

Edie laid her head against his chest. "I want that rotten killer to be brought to justice as much as you do.

But I wish . . . I wish someone else was going with you. I hate for you to try to capture him by yourself. He *is* riding with two other men, after all."

"I know," Colby assured her, patting her tenderly on the back, "but don't forget that I've been in this business all my life, honey. Don't you worry. I won't take any unnecessary risks. I arrested that mad dog once before, and I can do it again. As I told Bill Teague, I'm going to do my best to bring Malone in alive so he can face trial, but if he resists, I'll kill him. One way or another, I'm gonna get him."

Edie sighed. "I can't pretend that I'm happy about your decision, Colby, but I understand, and you have my support."

Colby kissed his wife with a sweetness born of equal parts of love, gratitude, and respect. "Thanks, honey. Just hold on to the same faith that you've had all these years that I'll come back safe and sound."

Releasing Edie, the sheriff went to pack his saddlebags, discovering that he was short on ammunition and would have to stop in town to replenish his supply. When he had finished his preparations, he gathered his family together and explained his mission to Nelda and his grandchildren. Then, telling them to watch for Jeff, he kissed each one, mounted up, and rode away. As soon as he was out of sight of the house, he reined in his horse. Taking the bullet-drilled badge from his pocket, he pinned it to his vest, half whispering, "I promise you, Son, that your death will be avenged. Duke Malone will pay for what he's done to us."

Reaching the former Daly ranch to try to learn the whereabouts of Marian and Ted Daly, Colby was informed by the new owner that three men had been there the day before, wanting the same information. When questioned, the rancher confirmed that one of the men answered Duke Malone's description.

"Were you able to give him an address?" Colby asked, feeling a chill run up his spine.

"No, Sheriff, I wasn't. Fact is, I don't exactly know where the Dalys have gone. Like I told those three yesterday, all I know is that Ted, Marian, and the kids moved to the general vicinity of Fort Worth, where they purchased a ranch."

Thanking the man, Colby spurred his horse and rode hard into Waco. When he reached the town, he immediately headed for Don Graham's gun shop, but before he got there, his attention was caught by a small crowd gathered in front of the funeral parlor. Trotting his horse over to the undertaker's, Colby slid from his saddle, tied his mount, and went inside.

"Paul?" he called. "It's Colby Tucker. What's up?"

"I'm back here, Colby," Paul Yelland answered from his back room. "And—seeing as how you're our sheriff again—I've got something I think you ought to look at."

Parting the curtains that separated the embalming room from the chapel, Colby found the undertaker examining a woman's body. The sheriff moved up beside Yelland and looked down at the corpse. "It's Lucille Deming!" Colby gasped.

"Yes. A couple of her neighbors found her. They had gone to her house to check on her as they did every other day or so. Found the back door kicked in and signs of a struggle inside. When they couldn't find Lucille in the house, they started looking around the yard. They found her floating in the well."

"I don't suppose it was an accident . . . I mean, could she have somehow slipped and fallen in?" the sheriff asked ruefully.

"I'm afraid not. I've sent for Doc to determine the exact cause of death, but even without any medical training I'd say the reason Mrs. Deming died is plain and clear. See these blue marks on her neck? She was strangled, sure as shootin'."

Pounding his fist into his palm, Colby swore. "And I'd bet my last dollar that I know who's responsible: Duke Malone. He probably went to the Deming house looking to kill Horace—and when that wasn't possible, he killed Lucille instead." Without another word he turned on his heel and hurried from the funeral parlor up the street to the gun shop.

While buying the ammunition he needed—several boxes of cartridges, including some .41-caliber rounds for the derringer he wore in a special pouch attached to the inside of his gun belt—he discussed with Graham the probable intentions of Duke Malone.

Colby stated, "He's obviously out to get anyone he figures did him wrong. I'm sure he's going to try to find Hans Brummer, too. Brummer's the one who put me on to Malone, you remember."

"Yes," Graham replied, nodding, "I remember. And I know where Hans is living now, too."

"You do?" Colby asked, surprised. "Where?"

"Wichita Falls. His brother Helmut came through town a few weeks ago. He's a lawyer in Wichita Falls, if you recall."

"Oh, that's right."

"Helmut told me Hans was living just a few blocks from him. He's married now. Owns a hardware store and is a model citizen."

"Glad to hear it," replied the sheriff. "Before I leave town, I'll send him a telegram and warn him that Malone is on the loose. As sly a cuss as that killer is, he's sure to find out where Hans is living."

"No doubt," agreed Graham.

"I'd like to send a telegram to the Dalys, too," Colby sighed, "but I don't have an address for them. I'll just have to ride hard and try to overtake Mad Dog."

"Yeah. Good luck, my friend. And at least you can head off knowing that Waco will have a lawman. Mayor Teague stopped by just a few minutes ago, said Wayne

Dunne got his leave of absence and is on his way over from Crawford."

"That *is* good news," Colby responded. "Thank goodness I won't have that worry while I'm gone." Hefting his package of ammunition, the sheriff turned to leave. "Well, see you when I get back."

"Be careful, old friend," cautioned Don Graham.

"I will be. I've already promised Edie that."

"I sure hope you get him, Colby."

"I'll get him," the silver-haired man said grimly. "That's a promise."

Chapter Five

It was a warm afternoon in Wichita Falls, Texas, and Margaret Brummer was finding it hard not to doze at her desk while working on the bookkeeping. The numbers in the fat ledger swam before her eyes, and finally, in exasperation, she closed the book and gazed out the window. *I guess I have an old-fashioned case of spring fever*, she told herself, amused at the thought. *And if Hans were here right now instead of in Chicago, I'd tell him we should leave the store in Darryl Schmidt's hands and go take a picnic basket out to some lovely spot and while away the afternoon.*

She was pulled back from her reverie by a sudden knock on her office door. "Yes?" she called.

"Mrs. Brummer, Ivan Olson, from the Western Union office, is here. He has a telegram for Mr. Brummer."

"Please tell him to come in, Darryl," she replied, standing to greet her visitor and automatically smoothing her shirtwaist and her strawberry-blond hair. Margaret Brummer, a stout, buxom woman in her early forties, was not at all pretty, but there was a sweetness about her that made everyone warm to her immediately.

"Afternoon, Miz Brummer," the old agent said, looking upset.

"Hello, Ivan," Margaret Brummer said kindly. "My

husband's away on business, but I can take the telegram for him. Who's it from?"

"Sheriff Colby Tucker, down at Waco," came the agent's reply as he handed over the yellow slip of paper. "It's very serious. It just came in over the wire, and I thought you'd better see it right away."

Concern touched Margaret's blue eyes. She had met and married Hans Brummer after he had been released from jail, and she had occasionally heard him speak of Sheriff Tucker. He admired the man even though he was the one who had arrested and jailed him.

Unfolding the telegram, Margaret quickly read the message:

> Mr. Hans Brummer, Wichita Falls, Texas. Be warned that you are in danger. Duke Malone has escaped Texas State Prison and intends to kill those responsible for his arrest. Has already murdered two. Certain you are targeted. Take every precaution. Colby Tucker, McLennan County Sheriff.

Margaret's face pinched with fear, and her plump cheeks paled to a chalky white. Putting out a hand to steady herself, she sank into her chair, thinking of what Hans had told her about Duke Malone. Before they married, the big husky German had revealed to her everything about himself, holding back nothing. He had been an outlaw and had ridden with the brutal and heartless Duke Malone, but within a short time Hans had realized the error of his ways and wanted to go straight. He was especially repelled by Malone's lust for killing and the low value he put on human life. Malone murdered people with less concern than a housewife swatting a fly.

Hans had told Margaret that when Sheriff Colby

Tucker arrested him, the lawman had given him an opportunity to cooperate with the state, telling him that if he led the authorities to where Malone was hiding out, the judge would be lenient with him. Hans had jumped at the chance for a shorter sentence, but mainly he wanted Malone to be caught and his senseless killing stopped. He told Tucker where Malone could be found, and Malone was subsequently captured. Certain that the killer would be executed, Hans did not worry about retaliation. After Malone was given a life sentence and carted off to the state penitentiary, Hans had often shared his fear with Margaret that Malone would break out and come after him. Lifting a trembling hand to her mouth, Margaret Brummer realized her husband's fears had been well founded.

Breaking the silence, Olson asked, "Does this killer know your husband lives here?"

Margaret blinked, then focused on the agent's wrinkled face and answered in a ragged, broken voice, "I . . . I don't think there's any way he could have found it out while in prison, but it won't be too hard to find out now." Looking at the agent, she said through quivering lips, "Oh, what am I going to do?"

"The best thing might be to talk to his brother, ma'am," offered Olson.

"You're right. I'm not thinking at all clearly." She stood up and came around the desk. As she put on her bonnet she told the agent, "Thank you for your concern, Mr. Olson—and for bringing the message so promptly. I do appreciate it. Come, I'll walk out with you."

Hurrying from the office and out of the store, Margaret Brummer dashed along the boardwalk to her brother-in-law's office. Ignoring his secretary, Margaret pushed open the door to his inner office and found the stout and muscular Helmut pulling a law book from his bookcase.

"Margaret, what's wrong?" he declared, immediately sensing her alarm. "Please, sit down."

Shoving the telegram in front of him, she said, "I'm too nervous to sit. Here, read this."

He took the telegram from her and read it, rubbing a worried hand over his clean-shaven face.

"What do you think?" she asked as he paced back and forth in front of her.

Looking intently at his sister-in-law, Helmut replied, "I think we've got to protect Hans. We've got to keep him from coming back to Wichita Falls until this Malone is captured or killed. I wouldn't feel confident of his safety in this town even if we surrounded him with bodyguards. When is he scheduled to leave Chicago?"

Margaret pondered the question for a few seconds, then replied, "Day after tomorrow."

"Then we've got to get a telegram to him immediately. He must not come home until Malone is caught."

The buxom woman shook her head. "I don't think he'll stay away, Helmut. He'll figure Malone might use me to get to him. If Hans thinks I'm in danger, his own safety won't matter. He'll come back as fast as he can."

"All we can do is try," said Helmut, worry etched on his face.

"Yes, you're right," Margaret agreed, nodding. "I'll go to the Western Union office right now and make sure the wire is sent immediately."

Staying off the main road between Waco and Fort Worth, Duke Malone and his partners forged ahead at a steady pace beneath the brilliant Texas sun. As they rode, Malone kept chuckling to himself. After a while Harry Blevins said, "Why don't you share the joke with us, Duke? We could use a good laugh."

"Ain't no joke, my friend," responded the killer. "I was just enjoyin' the thought of Colby Tucker bein' dead. Of course, I do have one regret about the whole thing."

"What's that?" queried George Niles.

"That Tucker didn't know it was me that killed him. I would like to have done it Indian style. You know . . . slow torture, with him lookin' me square in the face. It would have been a lot more satisfyin' if I knew he was aware that it was Duke Malone who took his miserable life."

"Well, at least *you* have the satisfaction of knowing he's dead and that you did it," put in Niles.

A few seconds passed, then Harry Blevins said, "Duke, I wouldn't for a moment want to spoil your pleasure, but something's been picking at my brain."

"What's that?"

"How do you know Tucker's dead? I mean, maybe the bullet didn't kill him. Maybe he's still alive."

Malone guffawed. "Are you joshin' me, Harry? Killin' is my business. I put that slug square through that badge pinned right above his heart. Don't you fret none. Ol' Colby Tucker is pushin' up daisies right now. The worms is gettin' ready to have themselves one hell of a big feast, and that's a fact." Throwing his head back, he laughed even harder.

They stopped at a brook to water their horses, and while the animals drank, the outlaws filled their canteens. When they were about to mount up and ride on, Malone commented, "Don't forget we've gotta be on the lookout for federal officers comin' after us. Some of 'em ain't too smart, but we'll keep our eyes open. We'll be all set once we collect that fifty thousand and head down into Mexico." Malone began chuckling to himself again.

"Enjoying thinking about the way you're gonna spend the money, eh, Duke?" Blevins asked.

"Naw," replied Malone, placing his foot in the stirrup. "I'm enjoyin' what's about to happen. I was just thinkin' how surprised my cheatin' wife's gonna be when she sets her eyes on me. Ol' Daly is gonna be a bit startled, too, you can bank on that. You talk about pleasure. Am I gonna have me a good time killin' them two!"

George Niles felt as though he had eaten something particularly repugnant. Duke Malone's passion for killing made him ill. Unable to keep silent about it one minute longer, he finally said somewhat tentatively, "Duke, you seem to enjoy killing."

"That's a fact," Malone agreed calmly. "What about it?"

"Well, I don't quite understand it."

"Few people do," chuckled Malone.

"I'm talking about the fun you seem to get from killing someone. It just isn't natural."

"It is for *me*," snickered Malone. "I like killin'. Hah! When I was a kid, I used to get a kick outta catchin' toads and squeezin' the life out of 'em. Ah . . . but killin' *people*—that's when the real thrill comes, especially when they've done me wrong. Snuffin' out their life sorta makes me feel like a god or somethin'."

Niles threw a quick glance at Blevins, and the look in Harry's eyes revealed that he too was feeling some revulsion. Pressing further, Niles said, "But what have the Dalys done that they deserve to die? I mean . . . you were sent to prison for life. Didn't your wife deserve a chance at happiness? It was only natural for her to want a husband. And it seems to me she needed a man to help raise your son and daughter."

Malone's mouth became a thin, angry line. Glowering at Niles, his drooping eyelid making the stare even more intimidating, the killer demanded, "What is it with you, George? You're beginnin' to sound like some damn preacher or somethin'."

Niles swallowed hard. "I'm hardly a preacher, Duke, but—"

"You don't like ridin' with me? Is that it? Let me tell you, pardner, you ain't gonna make no kind of outlaw bein' squeamish about sheddin' blood. You want out? Is that it?"

"It's not that, Duke," Niles said quickly. "It's just that I—"

"If you can't stomach it," cut in Malone, "why don't you just spur your horse in the other direction? Harry could probably find a place to spend your share of the money, ain't that so, Harry? And while you're ridin' back the other way, George, you tell them federal marshals I said hello, will you?"

George Niles's face went gray. He was in this thing up to his neck, and there was nothing he could do now but ride it out. He would talk to Harry privately and tell him they should both ditch Malone once they had their share of the fifty thousand dollars.

Niles looked at Blevins, then at Malone, and said, "I don't want out, Duke . . . but I just don't have the feelings you do about killing."

"How about if people we rob decide to shoot it out with us, George?" asked Malone. "You just gonna stand there and let 'em gun you down?"

"That'd be different," Niles promised. "That'd be self-defense. But cold-blooded murder . . . well, that's something else."

Malone grimaced, and for a fleeting moment Niles thought perhaps the expression was what the killer managed as a smile. "Don't worry, George," Malone declared, "I won't be askin' you to kill any of these people I'm after. I want that pleasure all for myself. Marian and her new husband get it, and then Hans Brummer gets it. After that we're gonna have us a high ol' time!"

"Where you gonna start looking for Brummer, Duke?" asked Harry Blevins.

"Wichita Falls," came the killer's answer.

"Why there?"

"He used to have a brother livin' there. Some kind of a fancy-pants lawyer. Maybe he's still there. If he is, a little pressure will loosen his tongue so's he won't mind tellin' me where Hans is. One way or the other, I'm findin' that rat. His days are numbered." Swinging into his saddle, Malone commanded, "Mount up, boys. We're gonna make us a quick stop in the town comin' up, then head out for Wichita Falls."

The two ex-guards eyed each other with concern. "I don't know, Duke," Niles said uneasily. "We agreed when we started out that it would be best to stay away from the towns. No sense in giving the law any kind of lead on our whereabouts."

"Well, I'll tell ya . . . I haven't tasted whiskey since before I was locked up in that stinkin' prison. I could really use a belt or two right now. Besides, Whitney ain't much of a town," argued Malone. "Probably no more than two hundred people in the whole place. But they've got a saloon, least they used to, and I'm mighty dry. We'll just go in, grab a couple drinks, and be on our way."

Niles did not like the idea that they might be seen. If they were caught, he and Harry would be back in Huntsville—only this time they would be inmates. Glancing at each other again, they shrugged and mounted their horses. They wanted that twenty-five thousand dollars, and they had to stick with Malone to get it. There was no choice; they would have to go into Whitney with him.

A short while later, as the three outlaws trotted along the main street, they saw immediately that the people in the small town were astir about something. Reaching the town's only saloon, they dismounted and tied their horses to the hitch rail. They stepped inside the saloon, pausing long enough to let their eyes adjust to the dimly lit room. A few men were seated at tables and several men were standing at the bar.

The threesome eased up to the bar. Malone, who stood closest to the door, put his foot on the brass rail and commented to the man standing next to him, "We're just passin' through, friend. Tell me somethin'. Folks around town seem a little excited. What's goin' on?"

"Indians," the man responded tersely, then tossed a drink down his throat from a shot glass.

"Whaddya mean?"

"The Comanches are on the warpath again. This morning they massacred an entire settlement about ten miles north of here. We're not feeling real safe right now. Those redskins might just get themselves a bigger war party and try wiping out our whole town next."

"This the first uprisin' in a while?"

"Yes. Started about three weeks ago. Other massacres have taken place all the way to the Oklahoma border along the Red River."

"Any idea what brought it on?"

Before the man could answer, the bartender approached, looked the three newcomers over, and asked, "What'll it be, gents?"

"Whiskey," came Malone's quick reply.

While the bartender was placing three glasses and a bottle on the bar, the customer turned to leave, answering as he did so, "What brought on the Indian troubles was the rough winter we had this past year. The Comanches were hit real hard. Lost most of their cattle. They've tried to trade handmade goods for cattle with ranchers like myself all over north Texas, but the ranchers have turned them down flat. Made them mad, so they're stealing cattle and killing whites at random."

The three outlaws glanced at each other, and then Duke Malone clapped George Niles on the shoulder, declaring, "I'm sure glad you two are ridin' with me.

One man alone out on the prairie would be a sittin' duck."

Niles smiled uneasily in reply, all the while thinking that the promise of easy money was in fact becoming less and less easy with every passing moment.

The men stood sipping their glasses of whiskey. Suddenly there was a raucous laugh, and two men came in, heading straight for the bar and standing next to Malone where the rancher had been. One of them had obviously been drinking already, and he was loud-mouthed and obnoxious. His companion ordered a drink and got it, but when the drunk told the bartender what he wanted, the bartender refused to serve him.

"Now listen, Frank!" the man yelled at the bartender. "I told you what I want. Lemme have it!"

The bartender eyed him with disgust and said, "Walton, you haven't paid me yet for the drinks I served you this morning—or yesterday either, for that matter—and until you pay up, you don't get any more liquor in here. You've had too much as it is."

The man cursed, then turned to his companion and asked him to buy him a drink, promising to pay him later.

"Forget it, Lester." The friend laughed. "I know you far too well. I'd never see that money again."

Swearing in disgust, Lester Walton turned to Duke Malone and said, "Hey, buddy! How's about loanin' me a few bits? I really need a drink."

Malone regarded him disdainfully. "I'm a stranger here, mister. If your friends won't trust you, why the hell should I?"

Bleary-eyed, Walton looked Malone up and down. Belching loudly he declared, "A man of means, wearin' two guns, and you won't buy poor Lester a drink?"

Malone fixed him with a scornful stare. "Get away from me, fella. I hate beggars."

Walton drew himself up to full height and said indignantly, "You, sir, are a ugly-faced, tight-fisted skinflint!"

George Niles stiffened as he felt the anger flare in Duke Malone. Without batting an eye the killer slapped Walton hard with an open palm, and the drunk staggered and fell to the sawdust floor.

Glaring at the man's friend, Malone asked, "You plannin' on interferin'?"

"Hell, no," the man replied, shaking his head. "I figure Lester had it coming. I've warned him about his drinking."

Suddenly Walton clawed for his gun as he raised up on one knee. Malone saw the move and kicked the gun from his hand. Whipping out his right-hand revolver, he thumbed back the hammer and pointed it between Lester Walton's suddenly terrified eyes. Malone rasped through gritted teeth, "If you know any prayers, you better say 'em quick, 'cause you're about to die!"

Walton's friend stepped close and said in a calm tone, "Wait a minute, mister—don't kill him. He's drunk. He doesn't know what he's doing."

Malone eyed the man coldly. "Drunk or not, he pulled a gun on me—maybe would've even killed me if I hadn't kicked the gun out of his hand—and let me tell you, nobody pulls a gun on me!"

Niles put a tentative hand on Malone's arm. Keeping his voice low and level, he reminded the killer, "We want to get to the river, don't we? You know what I mean."

"Yeah, sure. So what?"

"If you kill him, you're gonna put heat on us we don't need."

Malone turned and looked thoughtfully at his cohort. Nodding slowly, he said, "Okay, George. I guess you're right." With that he eased down the hammer and holstered the gun.

Lester Walton swallowed hard, wiping the sweat running down his face, and muttered a word only he understood. He started to get up when Duke Malone unexpectedly lashed out with his right foot and savagely kicked him square in the mouth. Walton flopped onto his back, blood bursting from split lips, and lay in the sawdust, moaning and spitting teeth.

"Let's get out of here," Niles urged.

"Yeah, let's," Malone sharply agreed. Tugging on his hat brim as he started toward the swinging doors, he turned and called to Walton's friend, "When he sobers up, tell 'im he's one damn lucky bastard. He's the only man who ever pulled a gun on me without dyin'."

The trio continued northward, riding hard through the afternoon. Happening onto a main road, Malone and his partners topped a gentle rise and saw a stagecoach about a quarter of a mile away coming toward them out of a shallow valley.

"Duke, there's too much traffic. Don't you think we better get off this road?" George Niles suggested as the coach neared. "We sure don't need to let everybody on that stage see us."

Harry Blevins asked wryly, "What difference does it make, after that bold appearance we made a few hours ago in Whitney?"

Malone glared at Blevins. "All them people was too busy worryin' about Comanches to worry about us," he answered sourly. But then he agreed with Niles, and the threesome began guiding their horses toward a tree-lined draw off to their left. They had gone only a few feet when they heard gunfire. Turning their horses around, they looked toward the oncoming stagecoach and saw a band of Indians closing in on it.

"What should we do, Duke?" asked Niles.

"Get down into these trees fast!" replied Malone. "If

you're thinkin' about helpin' out that stage, forget it.
There's too many redskins. Come on!"

The outlaws plunged their horses into the protection
of the trees, leaped from their saddles, left their mounts
ground-tied, then hurried on foot back to the edge of
the timber. Lying on their bellies, they watched the
Comanches shoot the shotgunner first. Apparently realizing there was no chance of outrunning the Indians,
the driver reined in the horses and set the handbrake.
From their vantage point the outlaws could see the man
pleading with the Comanches, but a moment later he
was shot in the head, blood gushing from his wound.
Then the Indians wrenched open the doors and began
pulling the passengers from the coach one by one.

"Duke, we've gotta help those people!" George Niles
whispered fiercely, feeling nauseated. He started to get
up, but Malone grabbed his left foot and yanked him
back down.

"Don't be stupid, Niles!" the killer hissed. "There's
too damn many of them savages, and *we'd* only end up
gettin' killed. Nope, the only killin' I aim to partake in
is what I'm doin' myself. Ain't nothin', or no one," he
growled, the threat evident in his voice, "is gonna hold
things up for me."

Niles kept his mouth shut, watching helplessly as the
Indians killed every one of the passengers. The Comanche
braves then unharnessed the horses and led them off
before setting the coach on fire. They rode away,
whooping with satisfaction.

As soon as the war party had gone, Malone and his
partners retrieved their horses and mounted up. As
they rode on to Fort Worth, Duke Malone turned to
George Niles and sneered, "See, Niles? I ain't the only
one who gets pleasure out of killin'."

"There's a difference, Duke," Niles responded somewhat incautiously. "The Indians were desperate, and
they were wronged by white people."

Malone laughed mirthlessly. "Ain't no difference, near as I can tell. I was wronged by some white people, too. And they're gonna get theirs same as those folks in that stagecoach did . . . only maybe not quite so quick."

Deputy United States marshals Clyde Zayre and Lowell Oldham arrived in Waco from the south, following Duke Malone's trail. At the same time Jeff Tucker rode in from the east, having received news of his brother's murder while en route to Nacogdoches. The three men drew up in front of the sheriff's office simultaneously and, eyeing each other's badges, exchanged greetings and dismounted.

Their spurs jingling loudly, the three men entered the office and introduced themselves to the man on duty. Jeff Tucker asked, "Is my father here?"

Acting Deputy Sheriff Wayne Dunne explained, "He left yesterday."

"Where'd he go?"

"He's chasing the man who killed your brother."

"You mean he knows who did it?"

"Yep. Duke Malone."

Jeff Tucker's mouth dropped open. "Duke M— You mean Mad Dog Duke Malone?"

"Yep. He broke out of prison. Came after your dad and got Jim instead."

U.S. Marshal Zayre spoke up. "Well, now, that's a coincidence. That's exactly why we're here. We're also on Malone's trail, and we stopped in Waco to see if anyone had seen him."

As Dunne was explaining what had happened, Mayor William Teague entered the office. "Howdy, Jeff," he interrupted. "Don Graham mentioned he saw you ride in, and I wanted to come see you. First of all, let me tell you how very sorry I am about Jim."

Jeff sighed, then answered softly, "Thanks, Mayor. I'm going to miss him."

"We all will. Which brings me to the other reason I wanted to talk to you. Would you consider becoming McLennan County's permanent sheriff, since your father's going to turn in his badge once he's brought in Malone? I've no doubt that in a special election, you'd get the nod of the people."

Jeff looked perplexed. "What about you, Deputy Dunne?"

Shaking his head, the deputy answered, "I'm just on loan from the town of Crawford. We didn't want your town to be without a lawman, so my marshal agreed to let me come on here temporarily."

"I see," Jeff Tucker replied. He was thoughtful for a long moment, then he told Teague, "I would be honored to take the position—and I'd like nothing better than to be back with my family again. But it'll have to wait till I return. I can't let my father try to bring in Malone by himself."

"The best thing to do, Tucker," U.S. Marshal Clyde Zayre told the young lawman gruffly, "is leave Malone to us—especially since he's got two other bad hombres riding with him."

"Then that's all the more reason for me to go," Jeff insisted.

"It's our job, Tucker," put in Oldham curtly, "and we'll handle it—a lot better than either you or your father could." Facing the mayor, the marshal asked, "Did anyone see which way Malone and his men headed?"

Nodding, Teague told him, "They were seen heading north."

"That's exactly what we figured," Oldham rejoined. "Probably wanting to find his former wife up around Fort Worth." Turning to his partner, he said, "Let's go, Clyde," and the two federal men hurried out and mounted up.

As he watched the marshals ride off, Jeff asked, "I presume my father headed in the same direction?"

"He did," Teague confirmed. "He's trying to overtake Malone and his two cohorts before they find where the Dalys are living."

"Thanks, Mayor," Jeff said, heading for the door.

As Jeff leaped onto his horse, William Teague called, "I'll hold the sheriff's position open until you've caught Malone."

"You do that!" Jeff shouted, then rode out of Waco.

The young lawman briefly stopped at his parents' home to comfort his family, and he also visited his brother's gravesite. Then Jeff Tucker rode hard, desperate to overtake his father before the sheriff, by himself, caught up with Mad Dog Malone.

Chapter Six

Nineteen-year-old Libby Malone pulled up in her buckboard in front of the general store in Fort Worth and reined in her docile bay. Setting the brake, the beautiful young woman glanced at the four young men who were loitering on a wooden bench in front of the store, feeling their eyes on her. With a toss of her long blond hair she gathered the skirt of her blue-and-white gingham dress, about to hop down from the wagon.

Suddenly the ogling young men scrambled to their feet, each one determined to be the one to help the lovely Libby from the wagon. Beating all the others to the side of the wagon, one of the men breathed, "Hello, Libby. May I have the privilege of helping you down?"

"Thank you, Lenny," she said coyly, batting her brown eyes and smiling at him while scooting to the edge of the seat. Lenny Carruthers reached up and encircled Libby's small waist with his powerful hands. Giggling, she allowed him to help her from the wagon.

After setting her down, Carruthers gazed longingly into her dark eyes and told her, "I'm glad you came into town. It saves me a long ride out to the Circle D."

"What do you mean?" she asked coyly, smoothing her dress.

Giving his friends a triumphant grin, he then looked down at the petite young woman and replied, "I was going to ride out and ask if you would accompany me to the barn dance Saturday night."

Libby smiled warmly at Carruthers and said kindly, "Lenny, I'm flattered that you want me to go with you, but we do live almost twelve miles from town, you know, and my stepfather wouldn't let me come to town without a well-armed escort because of the Comanches. So you see, it just wouldn't be possible for me to go to the dance—for I surely couldn't ask you to make such a long and dangerous journey by yourself just to escort me."

Keen disappointment showed on the young man's face. Suddenly he gave her a curious look and glanced around. Then he asked, "Did you have any such escort while driving into town just now?"

Gesturing with her chin, Libby responded, "Indeed I did. You don't see the eight ranch hands who rode with me because they're over at the stockyards right now. I'm to meet them there in a half hour for the trip back. They're from the Skyline Ranch—you know, the big spread about eight miles west of our place?"

"Oh," Lenny replied glumly, looking at the ground and kicking a small stone. Then he cocked his head and asked her, "Are you sure your stepfather isn't just being . . . well, mean or anything?"

Shaking her head vehemently, Libby responded, "Absolutely not. Ted Daly is the kindest, most tender-hearted man alive." Pausing, she said kindly but firmly, "I really must go now. I've got to purchase my supplies and then get to the stockyards so I don't hold up the Skyline men. But thanks again for the kind invitation. Maybe someday the Comanche threat will be over, and then we can take in a barn dance together." She smiled sweetly, then hiked up her skirt and stepped onto the boardwalk. Pausing at the doorway, she turned and gave Lenny a small wave before entering the store.

Inside, Libby Malone found three of her young lady

friends looking through the latest dress catalogue. They chatted briefly, then Libby made her purchases at the counter. When everything had been carried out to her wagon, she said good-bye to her friends, hurried out to the buckboard, and climbed in; then she headed for the stockyards.

At the same time Libby Malone was at the general store buying the goods her family needed, her outlaw father and his two companions rode up to the Fort Worth stockyards and dismounted. Between the shouts of the many ranchers and cowhands milling about and the bawling of the cattle in the pens, the noise was almost deafening.

Harry Blevins and George Niles stayed with the horses while Duke Malone moved through the crowd, looking for the office. Malone had explained to his cohorts that since Ted Daly had been a rancher when he lived in Waco, there was no reason to assume that he had changed professions when he moved. Figuring that as a rancher Daly no doubt did business at the stockyards, Malone was sure he would be able to find out the location of the Daly ranch.

When he stepped inside the office, a small group of cowhands stood talking with an imposing, well-dressed man. Aside from that group, there was a meek-looking man seated at a desk. Malone walked over to him and asked, "You in charge here, mister?"

"No, sir," replied the man timidly, looking up with a small smile. "I'm Mr. Blanchard's assistant. That's him over there talking with those gentlemen. Is there something I can do for you?"

Malone eyed him carefully, aware that the little man was a bit repulsed by his scars and droopy eyelid but was trying hard to hide it. "Maybe so," the killer finally answered. "I'm from down Waco way. A pal of mine moved from there to this area about four years ago.

Supposed to be ranchin' around here somewhere. Name's
Ted Daly. I figured he might do some business here.
You know him? I need directions to his place."

"Ted Daly?" repeated the little man. "Yes, I do know
him. He owns the Circle D Ranch—but to tell you the
truth, I have no idea where it is. Just a moment."
Looking toward the cluster of men, he called, "Mr.
Blanchard? . . ."

The important-looking man turned around. "Yes?"

"This gentleman is inquiring about Ted Daly. That is,
he's an old friend of Mr. Daly's, and he's wanting to
find his ranch. Can you help him?"

Web Blanchard excused himself from the cowhands
and stepped close to Duke Malone, appraising him
swiftly. "A friend of Ted's, eh?"

Malone was immediately aware that the stockyard
owner was suspicious of his looks—and particularly of
the tied-down holsters on his hips. Flicking a glance at
the assistant, then looking Blanchard in the eye, Malone replied, "Well, actually I'm Marian's brother. We've
sorta lost touch. I'm . . . uh . . . kinda the black sheep
of the family, truth to tell. But our pa died a few days
ago, and I need to let Marian know. Pa knew where
Ted and Marian are livin', but I don't. Could you tell
me how to find their ranch?"

The lie was apparently enough to convince Web
Blanchard. "Yeah," he agreed reluctantly. "The Circle
D is ten or twelve miles due west of Fort Worth. Take
the main road and just stay on it. You'll pass a deep
gulch that runs for about half a mile along the north
side of the road. When you reach the gulch, you're
about three miles from the Daly place. Just past the
gulch is a secondary road heading north. Take it for
another mile. You'll see the Circle D name on a gate."

"Much obliged," Malone replied tonelessly, turning
to leave.

"Hey, stranger!" called Blanchard just as Malone reached the door.

Malone halted and looked over his shoulder. "Yeah?"

"Give your sister my condolences."

"Sure will," lied Malone, nodding. He opened the door, stepped out, and closed it behind him. Chuckling to himself, the killer impatiently threaded his way through the throng and soon reached his companions, who looked at him nervously as though they were hiding something.

"Find out anything?" George Niles asked.

"Yep," Malone assured him. "Got me some good directions." Swinging into his saddle as the other two mounted up, he said, "You two can wait here in town. I want to handle this pleasure alone. Let's find you boys a saloon, and you can stay there until I come back. That way I'll know where to find you."

Ten minutes later Duke Malone was riding west out of Fort Worth, leaving his two companions standing in the doorway of the Big Texas Saloon.

After watching the killer hurry out of town, Blevins and Niles pushed their way through the swinging doors and sat down at a table. They ordered a bottle of whiskey, and when it arrived, Blevins popped the cork, poured their shot glasses full, and said, "Okay, George. Let's have that talk you said you wanted."

Looking around carefully to make sure no one could overhear them, Niles blurted, "I think we made a big mistake joining up with Malone, Harry. I've never known anybody could be so cold-blooded."

"I feel the same way," admitted Blevins. "It made me sick when Duke stuck the letter opener in the warden's throat—and it's only gotten worse since then. I knew, of course, that he set out to kill a number of people, but I somehow didn't think it would affect me the way it has. I mean, when he killed that old lady and threw her down the well . . ."

"Yeah, that really made me sick. And I'm afraid we're gonna see even more people killed who weren't on his list. I wish we'd never—"

"But we did, George," cut in Blevins. "We're accomplices now—and we need the twenty-five thousand. We've got to stay with him till we get our hands on the money. Then we'll play our cards right and ditch him at the right moment."

Relief spread over George's face. Easing back in his chair, he smiled and said, "I sure am glad to hear you say that, Harry! That's exactly what I was planning on doing. Okay, then, just as soon as we've got the cash, we'll leave Malone to his killing and head for somewhere far from Texas."

That afternoon Marian Daly stood leaning against the top rail of the corral fence with a Remington .44 rifle in her hands, which her husband had insisted she carry whenever she stepped out of the house. The still-beautiful middle-aged woman was watching her husband, Ted, and her twenty-two-year-old son, Rob. They were assisting a Texas longhorn cow birthing a calf, which was in a breech position. Glancing at the rifle, Marian grimaced. She hated having to carry it, but Ted was right: There was no way of knowing if the Comanches might show up, and it would be foolish to take unnecessary chances—especially since the Circle D Ranch was quite isolated. Like Marian, the two men were also armed, although their rifles were leaning against the barn, just inside the corral.

Putting such unsettling throughts from her mind, Marian refocused on Ted and Rob in their labors. She loved watching the two men work together, thinking they made a perfect team. Anyone who did not know otherwise would think they were really father and son, for although Ted had a red tinge to his hair and Rob's was dark brown, they were built much alike. She smiled to herself; they even moved in the same ways. Marian was glad Rob resembled his stepfather so closely. The less like his real father her son was, the better.

The cow lay on her side, eyes bulging and tongue hanging out, lowing loudly. She was obviously in great pain, but she seemed to understand that the two men were trying to help her. From where he knelt behind the cow, Ted called to his wife and said, "Honey, it's going to be a tough fight getting this calf out. Would you mind bringing a bucket of water? I'm going to need to keep washing my hands."

"Of course," Marian told him, pushing herself away from the corral fence and walking to the water trough halfway between the barn and the house. Leaning her rifle against the trough, she took the bucket from where it hung on the pump and dipped it full. Carrying both bucket and rifle, she hurried back to the corral, and her son reached over the top rail and took the bucket from her hand.

Looking past Rob, she called, "Ted, I'm going back in the house. I want to get some more work done on Libby's birthday dress before she gets home. Let me know when the calf is born, will you?"

"Don't worry, honey. You'll be the first to know—after Rob and me, of course."

Marian walked the hundred or so feet between the barn and the house, thinking about some touches she wanted to put on the dress she was making for her beloved daughter. Stepping onto the back porch, she gave a last glance back at the corral, then went inside. She sat down at her sewing machine, which had been placed in one corner of the large kitchen, and began pumping the foot pedal, picking up her dressmaking where she had left off. Hardly aware that she was doing so, she began humming a tune she had heard at the music hall a few weeks earlier.

Duke Malone reached the gate of the Circle D Ranch and read the name inscribed. Satisfied that he was finally going to get his revenge, he checked the loads of his pistols and turned onto the Dalys' road. As he drew near the house and buildings he noted the two men working in the corral. Judging by their ages, he had no doubt that the young man was his son, Rob, and the older man was the boy's stepfather. Cursing Ted Daly under his breath, Malone declared, "This is your last day on earth, cowboy."

Angling toward the house so as not to be seen by Ted and Rob, the killer rode up on the blind side of the house and dismounted. Then he stealthily made his way along the side of the house, still out of sight of the corral. He came to an open window, the afternoon breeze stirring the curtains, and as he drew nearer the window, Malone heard the whirring of a sewing machine and a woman humming happily.

Reaching the corner of the house, Malone glanced carefully around it. He could see the corral now, but the two men there were engrossed in helping a downed cow and were unaware of his presence. Stepping onto the back porch, Malone skulked to the door and quietly opened it. He peered inside and saw that Marian's back was toward him. Tiptoeing through the door, he entered the kitchen and crept toward her. She stopped working the sewing machine pedal just as the floor creaked under Duke Malone's step.

At the sound Marian twisted around in the chair, gasping loudly at the sight of her former husband. "Oh, my God!" she whispered hoarsely.

Malone's black eyes glared at her. "Well, if it isn't my faithful wife, Marian," he exclaimed coldly.

Her whole body shaking, Marian Daly pushed back the chair and stood up.

"What's the matter, *darlin'*," Malone asked, his voice dripping sarcasm. "Aren't you glad to see me?" He took another two steps, standing directly in front of her.

Marian's trembling fingers went to her gaping mouth. "H-how did you get out?"

"You don't think they *let* me out, do you?"

The woman's terrified eyes flicked toward the open kitchen door.

"You want to call 'em in?" he asked her through his clenched teeth. "Good idea. Go ahead." Whipping out both revolvers, he snorted, "I've got one gun for each."

Marian's eyes grew wider. "Duke! One of those men is your son! You wouldn't—"

"I will if he gets in my way."

Wringing her hands, Marian choked out the words, "Duke, l-listen to me. I'll run away with you. We can go right now. We can go out the front door. They won't see us, I'm sure of it."

Malone looked at her ferociously, and his cold eyes glinted. "Why would I want you to run away with me?"

"Well . . . I thought—"

"You thought wrong, Marian!" he lashed at her. "I don't want you within a thousand miles of me! I hate your two-timin' guts!"

"Then wh-why did you come here?"

She was shaking so badly that Malone thought she would collapse. Her terror was obviously growing with every passing second—just the way he had hoped. Ignoring her question, he dropped his guns in their holsters and gripped her shoulders with fingers like talons. He forced her down onto the straight-backed chair she had been sitting in at the sewing machine, and pointing a finger at her, he snarled, "You stay right there, woman!"

Marian began to weep while Duke Malone ransacked the kitchen cupboards. Tears spilled down her cheeks as she begged, "Duke, please, if you've got to take out your revenge on me, go ahead. But don't hurt Ted! He's been nothing but kind to your children. He's—"

"Shut up!" blared Malone, wrenching open doors and drawers, and leaving them as they stood. Finally he found what he was looking for. Picking up a roll of heavy twine, he pulled Marian's arms behind the chair and began wrapping the cord around her wrists. When he had finished binding them securely, he bound her ankles. Finally he tied the rope around her waist, securing her to the chair.

"Duke, please!" she begged. "Show some mercy for once in your life! Don't—"

Malone cut short Marian's plea when his right palm stung her face, whipping her head sideways. "You shut your trap!" he hissed.

"Duke, listen to me!" she cried.

Malone slapped her again, savagely hard. The impact of the blow knocked her over backward. Leaning down, he grabbed her by the shoulders and jerked her upright, and the chair settled under her weight. "I told you to shut your trap, didn't I?"

Marian's face bore a beet-red imprint of Malone's hand, and blood trickled from the corner of her mouth. "Please, Duke," she sobbed, "I beg of you, don't hurt Rob. He's your son!"

The muscles in his jaws twitched as Malone grunted, "I won't hurt Rob unless he forces me to. Where's Libby?"

"Sh-she's in town."

"When will she be back?"

"I . . . I'm not sure. But she's being escorted by eight cowboys. You'd better leave before they get here. They'll—"

The killer grabbed her by the shoulders again and shook her violently, causing the chair to rock. Marian's

lovely blond hair came loose from the pins that held it
in place.

"I'll leave when I get good and ready, woman!" he
railed, grabbing the back of the chair and yanking it
around so that she faced the back door. Looking out, he
saw Ted Daly and Rob Malone still kneeling beside the
cow. The killer drew a deep breath, then commanded
his ex-wife, "Now call your husband."

Looking up at him through her tangled hair, she
begged in a shaky voice, "Please don't do this awful
thing! Please, Duke!"

Leaning down, he gripped her face and pinched her
cheeks together, puckering her bloody lips. "I said call
your husband!" he growled.

Visible through the doorway, out in the corral, Ted
Daly and his stepson had just delivered the breech-
born calf. The newborn heifer was on her feet, staggering around, and the proud mother had risen to clean
her.

Picking up their rifles—Rob also toting the bucket—
the two men crawled between the fence rails and headed
for the house, triumphantly patting each other's back.
They had barely gone a few steps beyond the corral
when Marian's cracked voice came from the shadowed
interior of the kitchen, calling Ted's name.

Duke Malone stood behind Marian, chuckling evilly
as the two men came toward the house. Rob stopped
briefly to hang the bucket on the water pump at the
trough, then hurried to catch up with his stepfather.

When Malone drew his guns and cocked the hammers, Marian Daly screamed, "Ted! Look out! Duke's
here to kill you!"

Ted and Rob stopped in their tracks and looked at
each other for a split second, then charged the house,
their rifles held ready, apparently heedless of anything
except Marian's being in danger.

Malone circled around Marian, rushing to the door.

Taking aim at Ted Daly, the killer fired both guns, hitting Daly square in the chest. Marian screamed, and Rob raised his rifle. Before the young man could shoot, Malone took aim and fired at his son. Marian's agonized screams fairly echoed off the walls.

Winged in the shoulder, Rob Malone dropped the rifle and went down. The killer dashed out the door as Rob rolled on the ground, reaching for his rifle. Beating his son to the weapon, Mad Dog Malone snatched it up and threw it into the nearby water trough, then reached for Daly's rifle, throwing it in the trough as well. Standing over Ted Daly, Malone saw that the two slugs had done the job: Marian's husband was dead. Feeling great elation at having gunned down his enemy, the killer knelt and grabbed hold of Daly's arms and dragged the body behind some bushes around the far side of the house. Then he quickly returned to the backyard.

Rob gripped his wounded shoulder and struggled to rise, looking toward the kitchen and the sound of Marian's unending wails. As he gained his feet, the young man's eyes flashed with rage and he swore vehemently at Malone. Staggering toward him, he raged, "If you've hurt my mother, I'll kill you!"

Duke Malone felt his own fury rising, and his dark eyes flashed as he shouted to his son, "Don't you talk to me like that, boy! I'm your father!"

Rob turned on unsteady feet and started to totter toward the bushes where Malone had taken his stepfather, but he was too weak to take more than a step or two. Pivoting and staring fixedly at Malone, the youth said heatedly, "Ted Daly was more of a father to me than you ever were. I'd be mortally ashamed for anyone to know that someone as disgusting as you was my real father!"

Rushing toward his son, Malone punched the wounded young man with a powerful blow, knocking Rob to the ground. There was a maniacal gleam in the killer's eyes as he grabbed his bleeding son by the arm and dragged him into the house. Marian was sobbing incoherently as Malone pulled her son through the door and dropped him on the floor. Rob, his shirt soaked with blood, lay prostrate, shaking his head. Then he passed out.

Marian screeched at her ex-husband, her voice breaking with anguish, "You beast! You inhuman monster! How could you be so brutal toward your own son? If I could get my hands on you, I'd kill you! Do you hear me? I'd do the whole world a favor and send you back to hell where you came from!"

Holstering his guns, Mad Dog Malone reached out with his left hand, grabbed Marian's blond hair, and pulled her head back sharply. He brought his face close to hers and he bellowed, "It's all your fault, Marian! If you hadn't been so keen to leave me, none of this would've happened! You had no business divorcin' me and marryin' that wife-stealin' Daly." He leaned down, his face level with hers, and sneered, "Don't you remember our marriage vows, woman? You promised to honor and obey me, through sickness and health, till death do us part. Well, guess what, Marian? Death is about to part us. . . ."

Chapter Seven

Mad Dog Malone suddenly heard the sound of a group of horses at the end of the roadway. Going outside, he hurried to the side of the house and squinted into the distance. He saw a blond woman guiding her buckboard through the gate of the Circle D Ranch. On the main road, watching her, were a number of men on horseback.

Malone swore. "A posse!" he muttered. "They found me already!" He pulled out his guns, all the while realizing that he could not possibly win in a battle against so many men. The woman reined in her horse and, turning in her seat, waved to the riders. She then started up again and headed down the roadway toward the house while the men stood watching her passage. "I'll be damned," Malone said aloud. "They ain't no posse after all! That's gotta be Libby and the escort Marian talked about." As the buckboard drew closer, Malone realized that the blonde was indeed his daughter.

The killer raced back inside the house and hurried to Marian's side. Cocking his gun, he held it to her head and threatened, "Don't even so much as whisper a warnin', or so help me, I'll pull this trigger right now."

He watched through the half-open door, waiting for Libby to arrive. A few minutes later she drove in, stopping the wagon near the back porch and glancing toward the barn and corral. Seeing no one, she climbed

down from the buckboard and walked to the rear of the
wagon. She lifted out a box of groceries and, looking
toward the house, called, "Mother, Rob— I'm home!
Where is everybody? Would one of you please come
out here and give me a hand? We've got some bundles
to unload." Receiving no answer, she hefted the box
and stepped up on the porch, looking mildly piqued at
getting no help.

Walking through the back door, the young woman
halted in her tracks at the sight that greeted her: Her
battered mother was tied to a chair; her outlaw father—
who had been locked up in the penitentiary for six
years but whose cruel face she would never forget—was
standing beside her mother, holding her at gunpoint.
Her brother, lying on the floor, was bleeding profusely
from the shoulder.

"Oh, my God!" Libby Malone gasped, dropping the
grocery box. Dashing to her mother's side, she asked
breathlessly, "Mom, what has this brute done to you?
Oh, dear Lord, what does he want? Where's Dad?"

Smeared with blood and framed by her matted, di-
sheveled hair, Marian's face might have been a mask, it
was so distorted by both her fear and the beating she
had received. Her swollen lips moved, trying desperately to answer her daughter, but she could not get the
words to come.

Libby glared at her father and demanded, "How did
you get out of prison? Why have you done this to my
mother? Where's my dad? What has happened to my
brother?"

Malone holstered his gun and looked at his daughter
with admiration, saying, "You really turned out beautiful, kid."

At that instant Rob moaned with pain and started to
rise. Libby hurried to him, helping him to a chair.
Looking up at Malone, she railed, "*You* shot him, didn't
you! Why? Why have you done this?"

Regarding her blandly, the killer replied, "He was gonna shoot me. It was me or him."

"And my mother? Was she going to shoot you, too?" Libby snapped. She looked around the kitchen, then asked, worry creasing her forehead, "Where's Dad? What have you done to him?"

"He ain't your dad!" Malone shouted, his face red with sudden anger. "*I'm* your dad! If you're askin' about Daly, he's dead."

Libby's eyes filled with tears. She swallowed hard and asked softly, "Where is he?"

"Out there in the bushes—but you don't have to worry your pretty head about it." His voice growing colder, he ordered, "Sit yourself down in that chair next to your mother. I'm gonna tie you up so's you don't cause me no trouble. After all, I wouldn't want to have to hurt a sweet little thing like you."

Without warning, Libby dashed through the kitchen toward the parlor.

"You get back in here!" Malone called angrily, aiming the gun in her direction. He started across the kitchen after her, then halted when he saw Rob rise from his chair and go for a butcher knife that was sitting on the counter.

Swinging around in his son's direction, Malone aimed his gun and fired it just after Rob threw the knife. The blade flew across the room and buried itself in the killer's upper left arm.

The slug hit Rob in the chest, and he bounced against the cabinet and collapsed. Swearing loudly, Malone staggered across the kitchen to see if Rob was dead. From the corner of his eye he saw Libby in the doorway, aiming a Colt .44 at his head.

Her eyes were wild as she barked, "Drop the gun, Duke!"

Malone thumbed back the hammer on his revolver and whirled. A bit off balance, he fired at Libby. The bullet grazed her left temple and she dropped to the floor unconscious. Cursing his traitorous children, Malone holstered his gun, and gripping the handle of the butcher knife, he yanked it from his arm. Blood spurted from the wound, soaking his shirtsleeve.

Marian's screams and curses rang in his ears as he turned and looked down at his son lying motionless on the floor, apparently dead. Breathing heavily, he gritted his teeth against the pain in his arm. Then he focused on his former wife and slowly plodded toward her. Looking at her with uncontrolled hatred, he raised his arm and cursing her for having borne two such disloyal children, plunged the butcher knife into her heart. Her eyes opened wide and she stared at him as if in surprise. The stare became fixed, and after a moment the eyes were unseeing. "Good-bye, Marian," Malone hissed. Then he shoved the chair over backward, and she slumped heavily on her back, her blank eyes staring at the ceiling.

Hurriedly the killer ransacked the cabinet drawers until he found a linen napkin. He wrapped it around his arm as a tourniquet to stop the bleeding, tying a knot with his good hand and teeth. Pushing out the spent cartridges in both his revolvers, he reloaded them and was about to leave when he thought he heard Libby stirring.

Malone went and looked down at her. She remained motionless. He thought of putting another bullet through her, but then he thought better of it, for he heard a noise from outside—it could be an animal, or possibly those men who'd accompanied her, returning to check up on things. Silently he wheeled and bolted out of the house. He was satisfied that Marian and her husband were dead, and he was eager to rejoin Blevins and Niles and head for the Red River. The fifty thousand dollars was waiting.

*   *   *

Libby blinked her eyes and slowly sat up, then waited for the room to stop spinning. When her vision cleared, she saw her mother lying on the floor, still tied to the overturned chair, with the butcher's knife buried in her chest.

"Mama," Libby whimpered softly. "Oh, Mama . . ." Tears flooded Libby's eyes as she hurried to Marian. "Don't be dead . . . oh, Mama, please don't be dead! Please, God, don't take her away from me . . . please!" Her body was racked with sobs at the sight of her mother's unseeing eyes. Rocking like a child, she sat hugging herself tightly, as if seeking comfort from her own touch.

Finally turning away from the terrible sight of her dead mother, she saw that her brother was still breathing, and hope rising, she crawled to him. Libby steeled herself and looked closely at his bloodied shirt, finding that the bullet had hit him on the right side of the chest, missing his heart. "Rob? Rob, can you hear me?" she asked anxiously.

Her brother opened his eyes and looked at Libby, pain evident on his face. "Is . . . is he gone?" he whispered, his voice barely audible.

Libby's face was twisted with grief as, nodding, she answered, "He's gone, Rob. But he killed Mother."

Tears flooded the young man's eyes, and he struggled to sit up.

"No! Don't try to move," Libby commanded. "Just stay still while I get some bandages." The young woman stood up, reeled for a moment, then carefully made her way to the cupboard where the family kept some medical supplies. Grabbing some bandages, she then went to her room and took the pillow off her bed. She hurried back to the kitchen and put the pillow under Rob's head, then wrapped his chest with the bandages to try to control the bleeding. After making her brother as comfortable as possible, she sat there on the floor next to him, caressing his face as she would a child's.

Glancing toward the window, she realized the sun was about to set. Even were it not for the Comanche threat, it would not be possible to ride into Fort Worth and get the doctor, for soon it would be dark. Suddenly she remembered Ted Daly's body lying outside in the bushes. Tears sprang anew into her eyes as she thought of the gentle man she had called father for more than five years—now dead at the hands of her real father. *I can't leave his body out there for the animals to get,* she told herself, and she stood up.

When she did so, her knees almost buckled under a wave of dizziness. She felt a thin trickle of blood on the side of her face and remembered the bullet that had creased her head. When the dizziness subsided, she crossed the kitchen to the cupboard and rummaged inside until she found the bottle of tincture of iodine, and gritting her teeth against the pain, she applied some to her wound. Satisfied that she had done enough for herself, she focused again on her family.

She checked on Rob once more, then steeled herself for what she had to do next. As though pushed by some unseen hand, Libby went over to her mother. Taking the scissors off the sewing table, she cut through the cords that bound Marian Daly to the chair. Closing her eyes and swallowing hard against rising nausea, she gripped the handle of the knife and pulled it out of her mother's chest. Then she ran to her room, dragged the chenille spread off the bed, and returned to the kitchen. As tears coursed down her cheeks, she gently covered her mother's body.

Wiping her cheeks with the backs of her hands, she knelt by her brother and told him she would not be gone long, then hurried outside. Libby followed the footprints in the dirt and found where Duke Malone had hauled the lifeless form of Ted Daly. Although weak from her ordeal, she took hold of Daly's wrists and began dragging him toward the house. By the time she reached the porch, she was exhausted. Leaving Daly's body by the steps, she sat down on the porch, gasping for air through unrelenting sobs.

After a few moments she rose to her feet and glanced at the lowering sun, then went to check on her brother. Rob was still conscious, but he was losing blood and weakening. "Sis," he whispered, "you've got to help me. I'm . . . pretty sure the first . . . bullet, the one . . . that hit my shoulder, passed . . . through, but if the slug . . . in my chest isn't dug out . . . right away, I'll die."

Libby was in a frenzy. Clenching her fists, she said, "Rob, I don't think I can do it. I've never even *seen* a bullet wound before, much less removed a bullet. If . . . if I try, and do something wrong, it will be *me* who kills you."

"I'll . . . die anyway if . . . you don't try," choked Rob.

Libby put her fists to her forehead and whimpered. Even if she could reach Fort Worth in the dark and got the doctor, Rob would be dead before they returned. Then she thought of the Skyline Ranch. There had to be someone there who had dealt with gunshot wounds. But then she realized that by the time she saddled a horse, rode to the neighboring ranch, and returned with help, her brother would no doubt be dead. Rob was right; she had no choice.

Cradling his cheek with a shaky hand, she said, "All right, Rob. I'll do my best."

"A fella . . . can't ask . . . for any more than . . . that," he assured her.

Libby stood up, trying to calm herself and think clearly. She knew the knife she would use to probe for the slug must be sterilized; she knew also that the wound would have to be sterilized when the slug was removed, before she stitched it up. That meant she would need some wood alcohol, needle and thread, a narrow-bladed knife, and more bandages.

She had methodically collected the items she needed for the operation and was about to start washing her hands when she heard hoofbeats on the roadway, heading toward the house. Her heart started pounding and she felt the blood drain from her face. "Dear God," she whispered aloud. "Don't let it be Duke!"

She ran for the revolver, which still lay where it had fallen from her grasp, and then she positioned herself beside the back door, just out of sight. She heard the rider dismount and cross the yard, pausing at the porch. Then the floorboards creaked. Holding her breath, her gun trained on the doorway, she waited for her visitor to walk in.

"Sheriff Tucker!" she exclaimed at the welcome sight of the lawman she had not seen for four years but whom she recognized immediately. The sheriff, too, was holding his gun, and they both sighed with relief as they put down their weapons.

"Oh, Sheriff Tucker!" she breathed, her tears beginning anew. "I'm so glad to see you! Duke Malone was here. He . . . he killed my mother and my dad. And Rob's been shot in the chest, but he's still alive."

The sheriff crossed to Libby and enfolded her in his arms. "Oh, my dear girl, I'm so sorry. . . . I've been on Malone's trail, Libby, and I'd hoped to catch up to him before . . . before this happened." He was silent for a moment. "He killed my son Jim a few days ago," he added solemnly. "Thought he was killing me. I guess he still thinks he did."

Hope welled up in Libby. Sniffing loudly, she asked, "Sheriff, have you ever dug a bullet out of someone?"

Nodding, the silver-haired lawman replied, "I have. Not something I'm comfortable doing, though."

Leading him to where her brother lay on the kitchen

floor, she begged, "You've got to help him! I don't think I can do it."

Tucker took off his hat, tossing it on the kitchen table, and knelt down beside Rob Malone. "Howdy, boy," he said, trying to sound confident.

Rob looked up at the sheriff and said, "I knew . . . your voice . . . the moment . . . I heard it. Sure . . . sure am glad you're . . . here."

"Let's take a look at these wounds," Colby told him softly, pulling back the blood-soaked bandaging.

"What do you think?" Libby asked after a moment.

Tucker shook his head. "The slug that hit his shoulder seems to have passed on through, but the one in his chest—well, it's pretty bad. He needs a doctor, honey."

"You know how far it is to Fort Worth and back, Sheriff. I don't think there's time."

Colby stroked his mustache and said, "You're right. That'd take too long." Sighing, he said, "I guess it's up to me, then, isn't it?"

"Oh, bless you!" Libby sobbed.

Looking around, he asked, "You got any whiskey?"

"Yes."

"Get as much down Rob as fast as you can. There's no way to do this without hurting him a whole lot, but the whiskey will help dull his senses some." He looked around. "How about lye soap?"

"Over there by the wash basin. In that white dish."

"Okay," Colby responded, rolling up his sleeves and crossing the room.

Libby knelt beside her brother and began giving him whiskey from a nearly full bottle. Rob choked and coughed, wincing with the pain the movement brought, but Libby kept pouring it down while Colby Tucker washed his hands.

When a third of the whiskey was gone from the bottle, Rob gagged and said, "That's all I can take, Sis." His throat burned and his eyes were watering.

Looking over his shoulder, the sheriff told Libby,

"Okay. That's enough. Don't want to make him sick."
He finished scrubbing his hands. "Libby, come here
and help me. Pour that wood alcohol over my hands.
Then find me a knife with a wide blade. I'll be using
that slender one, but I'll need a wide one, too. You see,
I'm afraid thread won't be enough. In order to stop the
bleeding when that slug comes out, we'll have to cau-
terize the blood vessels—which means searing the flesh."

Libby felt sick all over again.

"While I'm digging," Colby continued, "you hold the
wide-bladed knife in the lamp flame. I want it red hot."

Wincing at the thought, she assured the sheriff that
she would do her part. Then she poured the alcohol
over his hands, and Colby knelt down beside Rob
Malone.

The lawman picked up the knife with the sharp point
and said with a steady voice, "This is going to hurt,
Rob. It's going to hurt a lot. Are you ready?"

Sweat already beaded Rob's brow. "Yeah," the young
man managed to whisper.

The room was growing darker, and Libby lit the lamp
hanging over the kitchen table. The room was immediately bathed in light, but Colby told her, "Can you
bring another lamp? I'll need more light than this. Set
it up here on the sewing table."

Libby complied. Then, while Colby Tucker went to
work with one knife, she held the other in the flame of
one of the lamps. Rob screamed in agony as the sharp
knife probed into his flesh, losing consciousness just
before the bullet was removed. Grabbing the red-hot
knife from Libby's hand, Colby immediately cauterized
the wound in Rob's chest, and the one in his shoulder
as well, and then they both bandaged the wounds.

Rob remained unconscious, and Colby studied his
face and told Libby, "He's in mighty serious condition,
honey. I have to be honest with you . . . I'm afraid his

chances aren't good. I've done all I can, but that may
not be enough."

Libby felt as though her own chest had been pierced.
Biting her lip as tears resurfaced, the young woman
stared in anguish at her brother. She drew a shuddering breath and replied, "He's all I have left, Sheriff. If
Rob dies, I'll be completely alone." Looking up at the
lawman, she asked in a tiny voice, "Will you be going
off now after Duke Malone?"

Colby looked into the young woman's eyes, reading
there the unspoken plea, and wrapped his arms around
her. "Don't worry, Libby. As much as I need to catch
up with that maniac—forgive me, I know he's your
father—I won't leave you at a time like this." Releasing
her, he said, "Let's let your brother rest now."

Colby Tucker went to the basin and pumped the well
handle. As he washed the blood from his hands, Libby
stepped up beside him and murmured, "Thank you,
Sheriff Tucker, for all your help. I don't know what I'd
have done if you hadn't shown up."

"You'd have done exactly what you needed to, girl,"
he said sincerely. "You're a mighty strong young woman,
I can tell."

The welling tears spilled down her cheeks. "I d-don't
feel very strong," she sobbed. Reaching for Colby Tucker,
Libby Malone clung to the old lawman, and all the grief
and fear she had been holding in check rushed out,
overwhelming her. When her racking sobs finally subsided, she smiled wanly at Colby. "Forgive me. You're
feeling just as much sadness as I am. Your Jim—"

"There's nothing to forgive, child. Come. Why don't
we go sit down?"

"You must be hungry," she realized with a start.
"You've been riding for hours, and then you helped
Rob. . . . I'll fix you something to eat."

"Don't go to any bother, Libby," Colby responded.
"I don't need anything."

"Sure you do," she contradicted, attempting to put a lilt in her voice. "And when Rob comes to, I'll give him some broth."

Nodding, the lawman admitted, "I guess I could use a little something. Tell you what, while you're seeing to the food, I'll—" He paused, as if not wanting to finish his thought. "I'll see to your stepfather."

Libby hung her head briefly. "Thank you," she murmured. "I'd almost forgotten. . . ." She threw a quick glance toward the blanket-covered form of her mother, shuddered slightly, then distracted herself by preparing a light meal for the sheriff and herself.

Colby Tucker reentered the house a few minutes later, carrying the body of Ted Daly. "I'll take your stepfather's body into another room," he told Libby, "and then I'll do the same with your mother. I think it might be a little easier for you then."

Wordlessly nodding her thanks, Libby kept her eyes averted when Colby came back into the kitchen for Marian Daly's body. A few moments later Libby heard the door to her parents' bedroom close, and she was incredibly thankful for the sheriff's presence.

"You can go for the local sheriff and the undertaker tomorrow morning," Colby Tucker told her as he sat down at the kitchen table.

"I'm so grateful for your help, Sheriff Tucker. I don't know how to thank you."

He smiled tenderly at her. "You can thank me by sharing some of that good-smelling food with me."

Shaking her head, she insisted, "No, I couldn't."

"Yes, you can—and you must. You've got quite an ordeal ahead of you, young lady, and you're going to need all the strength you can muster."

Libby sighed. "I guess you're right," she admitted, taking another plate and some silverware from a cupboard.

Sitting across from each other, they ate silently, each

lost in thought. Finally breaking the silence, Colby asked, "Do you kids have any other relatives nearby?"

Libby looked up from her plate and replied, "Not nearby. We have an uncle and aunt back east—but I have no idea where they live. We haven't kept in touch with them. I think they're in Ohio." As she spoke, she noticed for the first time the hole in the sheriff's badge. "Is that—?"

"Yep," he replied. "It's a bullet hole."

"You were shot *there* and you're still alive?"

He shook his head. "No," he answered softly. "My Jim was wearing this badge when your fa—when Duke Malone murdered him, thinking he was murdering me." He paused, swallowing hard. "You see, Jim took over my job as McLennan County's sheriff—in fact, I had retired that very day. Jim had served as my deputy for the last five years, and he was voted in as sheriff upon my retirement." He added bitterly, "I've taken my old job back for the sole purpose of hunting down the man who murdered my boy. I'm wearing this badge because the last act I will perform as McLennan County sheriff will be bringing in or killing Duke Malone."

"It shames me to know that Duke Malone is my real father," Libby said ruefully. "When I think of all the people he has murdered—"

"It's got nothing to do with you, honey," Colby assured her. "You're not responsible for his actions. You can't help who your father is or what he does."

"I know," she agreed sadly. "I just wish he weren't my father." She stared past him, unseeing, for a long moment. Then, changing the subject, she asked, "You have another son, don't you? About my age?"

"Yes, that's right. Jeff. He's a few years older than you, I believe." Colby smiled, then told her proudly, "He's a lawman, too. Town marshal of Nacogdoches, though I'd be right glad if he could take over in Waco."

"Upholding the law runs in the family, I see." She tried to smile.

"I guess it does."

Giving up on small talk, Libby once again fell silent, focusing on her plate of food. After a few bites she stood up and left the table to check on Rob. He was breathing evenly but shallowly. She walked back to the table, standing beside the lawman. "I think he's just sleeping now, and not unconscious," she told him, feeling somewhat hopeful. "Probably the effects of the whiskey."

"That's good."

Suddenly her tragedy all came rushing back. Feeling utterly forlorn, she moaned, "Sheriff Tucker, Rob just *has* to live." She broke down, covering her face with her hands.

Colby Tucker stood up and folded her into his arms, holding her head against his chest. "Go ahead, darlin'," he told her gently. "Just cry it all out. Then you should try to get some sleep yourself." He sighed, adding, "I know it's the usual thing to say, 'Things'll look a whole lot brighter in the morning' . . . but I'd be lying if I were to promise you that."

Chapter Eight

The gray light of dawn crept over the Texas prairie, and as the birds in the copse of tall oak trees set up a chatter to greet the day, deputy U.S. marshals Clyde Zayre and Lowell Oldham stirred in their bedrolls.

Oldham was the first to awaken fully. Blinking against the lightening sky, he then focused on the outstretched limbs of the trees overhead, sleepily watching the chattering birds fluttering from perch to perch. He sat up, rubbed the sleep from his eyes, and gazed around. Their horses stood silently and patiently where they were tethered on the nearby creek bank, and a light breeze carried wisps of low, curling mist above the grassy prairie.

Zayre rolled over in his bedroll and looked at his partner. "Oh, you're awake, too, eh? Guess it's time to crawl out and get with it."

"Yep. You want to build the fire and make breakfast or feed and saddle the horses?"

"Makes no never mind to me," replied Zayre, sitting up and stretching.

"Okay," Oldham decided, "in that case, I'll get the fire going while you get the animals ready to travel."

Minutes later the two lawmen sat down on a log next to the fire and began eating their breakfast. Through a mouthful of ham and beans Oldham said, "You *have* faced the fact that we aren't gonna get ahead of Colby Tucker, haven't you?"

Zayre swallowed and answered, "Yeah. The man's got a reputation for being a bloodhound when it comes to trailing outlaws under any circumstances—but when it comes to the man who murdered his boy, why, he'll be hotter on Malone's heels than a hound after a rabbit. I sorta figure we'll meet Tucker coming back with all three of them in tow."

"You think they'll be alive?"

"Blevins and Niles probably will be, but I don't know about Malone. He may be draped over his horse."

Oldham sipped the steaming coffee in his tin cup, then said, "I don't think we'll have any trouble getting Tucker to turn the two accomplices over to us. And if that *is* the case with Malone, then we won't have anything to worry about."

Zayre chuckled. "I know what you're thinking. If Tucker is bringing Malone in alive . . . will he let us have him?"

"Exactly."

"He'll have to. Malone murdered Warden Alton and broke out of Texas State Prison. That makes it a federal case—which means it's *our* job to bring him in."

"Tucker may not see it that way. Hell, you know the old saying about blood being thicker than water. If you were Tucker, wouldn't you want the privilege of slipping the noose over that bastard's head?"

"Sure would," agreed Zayre. "So I guess what you're saying is we'd best be prepared to butt heads with the sheriff."

"Yep. That's what I'm saying . . . *if* Malone isn't already dead when we meet up with Tucker."

"Just between you and me, my friend," Clyde Zayre confided, "I hope he is."

"Yeah," sighed Oldham, "me t—"

A distant hissing sound ended abruptly with a sodden thwack, and Marshal Lowell Oldham grunted and fell forward into the fire. There was a feathered arrow sticking from between his shoulder blades.

Clyde Zayre dropped his tin plate and clawed for his revolver as the peaceful morning air was suddenly split with a series of wild war cries. Three arrows hit Zayre at the same time. He staggered and fell on his back, still attempting to bring his gun into play as half a dozen painted Comanche warriors closed in on him. A fourth arrow ripped through his throat, pinning his body to the ground.

With loud, jubilant whoops the war-painted Indians quickly went to work with their knives. A couple of them pulled Oldham's body from the fire, and one brave took his scalp, while another did the same to Zayre. The two Comanches held the bloody scalps high over their heads and laughed victoriously, and then the warriors dashed to their horses that were hidden along the creek bank nearby.

Less than an hour after the Comanche attack, Jeff Tucker went to water his horse at the same creek and came upon the grisly scene. The young lawman swore as he reined in and swung from his saddle. Stepping to the arrow-riddled body of Clyde Zayre, Jeff's stomach turned when he saw the bloody mass where Zayre's scalp had been. He turned away and breathed deeply for a few moments, fighting his nausea. Then he went to check on Lowell Oldham and found him in the same condition as his partner.

Jeff was surprised that the Indians had not bothered to take the lawmen's horses, but it made his task easier. Snapping off the arrows in the bodies, he wrapped the men in blankets and draped them over their saddles. He led the horses into the next town and turned the bodies over to the local marshal, who volunteered to contact the U.S. marshal's office in Austin. Explaining that he was in a hurry, the tall, lanky marshal of Nacogdoches quickly rode on.

*   *   *

As daylight slowly filtered into the kitchen of the Daly ranch house, Sheriff Colby Tucker quietly leaned over and pulled the blanket over Rob Malone's face. Then he silently watched the still-sleeping Libby Malone, noting how even in sleep her lovely face wore a troubled, sad expression. She had insisted on sleeping beside her wounded brother, whom they felt it best not to move, and after a brief argument Colby relented and carried a small mattress into the kitchen so that at least she would be comfortable. But Libby had not gone to sleep until well after two o'clock in the morning, and only then because Tucker had promised to stay awake and watch over Rob, and to rouse her if there was any change.

He was not sure when the young man had died because he had kept the lamp burning low. Now, in the growing light, he could see that Rob had in fact stopped breathing, but he decided against waking Libby. *I know I promised to let you know if there was any change, little gal, but since you're going to hurt even more when you wake up, I'm going to let you sleep as much as you can.*

Easing back onto the hard, straight-backed chair where he had been sitting all night, Tucker took a deep breath and let it out slowly, thinking about how Libby was going to deal with this latest blow. He studied the bullet burn on Libby's temple, remembering how he had thought it was some kind of bruise suffered during the ruckus with her father—then finding out that Malone had shot at her. *Dear God,* thought Colby, *what kind of vile beast could turn a gun on his own son and daughter?* Shaking his head, he whispered, "Some kind of life you've known, you poor little thing . . . and now you've been robbed of your entire family."

A calf bawled somewhere out beyond the barn, and the throaty answer from its mother came in reply. Colby's thoughts ran to his family. There were two little

children without a father now—and Nelda was a widow.
Edie's heart was badly torn over the loss of her oldest
child, and Jeff would suffer deeply because of his brother's death. It was almost inconceivable that all of this
horrible pain and grief had been caused by one heartless, cold-blooded excuse for a human being.

As he thought of Jim, suddenly numerous memories
flooded through Colby Tucker's mind. He relived the
day Jim was born and the pride he had known holding
his firstborn son. Other scenes flashed before his mind's
eye—boyhood adventures, the day Jim and Nelda were
married, the day Jim first became his deputy, the times
he had made his father so proud when he courageously
faced danger and death and proved he was worthy of
wearing a badge. Then came the memory of that moment a few days before when Colby had pinned his own
badge on Jim . . . not knowing that the shiny piece
of metal would become a target for Duke Malone.

Abruptly fury exploded inside Colby Tucker, and he
felt hatred like he had never known in his sixty years.
His weathered face took on an expression of uncontrolled rage. Clenching his fists, he put his head on his
knees and breathed slowly through gritted teeth, trying
to bring his fury under control. Colby Tucker had killed
many an outlaw in his years as a lawman, but only when
he had to and always in the line of duty. At that
moment he wanted desperately to rip off the badge,
throw it away, and go after Malone with all the fury of a
wronged and vengeful father.

Colby's tense body suddenly went limp. *You're wearing a badge, remember? You took an oath. You're bound
by your word to uphold the law, not take it into your
own hands. You must capture Duke Malone alive if
possible and let the law take its course.*

Mopping the sweat on his forehead with his sleeve,
the sheriff of McLennan County thought, *I'll wear this
badge until justice has been done—then I'll throw it
away.*

A finger of sunlight poked through one of the kitchen windows, and Colby doused the lamp. Looking down at Libby Malone, he told her silently, *You poor kid. Usually the sunrise brings cheer after a long, agonizing night—but not this time. For you, it'll only bring more sorrow.*

It was as if Colby's thoughts touched Libby's mind. She stirred and moaned, thrashing about slightly, then opened her eyes. Gazing at the lawman, she smiled wanly, saying softly, "Good morning, Sheriff. How's Rob?"

Colby stiffened, and Libby accurately read his movements. Jerking to a sitting position, she looked over at where her brother lay. When she saw the blanket covering his face, she whimpered, "Oh, no!"

"I'm sorry, little gal," Colby said tenderly, kneeling down beside her. "But at least he went easy. Just died in his sleep."

All the color drained out of Libby Malone's face. Tears rushed to her eyes, and then she seemed to cave in. Tucker gathered her into his arms, and she clung to his neck, sobbing piteously.

Thinking it best to get her away from the body of her brother, Colby tenderly picked her up and carried her out of the house. He set her down on the edge of the porch, then sat down beside her, his arms around her, speaking to her softly and soothingly.

They had been huddled together on the porch for nearly ten minutes when Colby caught movement on the roadway from the corner of his eye. They were about to have a visitor. Shifting his head slightly, he tried to get a clearer view of the rider, but the house was angled in such a way that soon after he had seen him, the man disappeared from his line of sight, behind the house. Stiffening, his hand automatically going toward his revolver, the lawman waited.

The clip-clopping of the horse's hooves got louder

and the man came closer. Then the horse's head became visible around the edge of the house. "Jeff!" Colby exclaimed, recognizing the horse and breathing with relief.

"Hi, Dad," the young marshal said a moment later, his face somber. "I'm glad I was able to find you." Dismounting, Jeff tied his horse to the hitching post, then walked to the house. He removed his hat and smiled sadly. "Hello, Libby. It's been quite a while, hasn't it?"

Libby Malone lifted her head from Colby's shoulder and wiped away her tears with the back of her hand. Sniffing, she turned and faced Jeff Tucker. "Hello, Jeff," she said quietly.

"I'm sorry we had to meet again under such terrible circumstances."

She looked away from him. "So am I," she murmured.

Colby Tucker slipped his arm off Libby's shoulder and stood up. Embracing his son, he asked, "I guess my sad news caught up with you well before you reached Nacogdoches."

Pulling away from his father, Jeff nodded and replied, "Yeah, the marshal in Groesbeck told me. I'm sure glad I stopped in to pay my respects to him as I rode through his town."

"But what are you doing here, boy? I figured you'd go home and comfort your mother."

Turning his hat around in his hands, Jeff responded, "I did go home. Briefly. But I figured my place is here with you, Dad. I came to help you bring in Malone. Has he been here?" the young man asked, looking from his father to Libby.

Colby breathed heavily. "He sure has," he finally replied. Gesturing with his head toward the house, he explained, "Son, Libby's family—her mother, her stepfather, and her brother—are all dead. She's lucky to still be alive herself. Her father shot at her, but fortunately the bullet only grazed her."

The young woman began weeping. "I don't feel at all fortunate," she wailed, looking utterly lost.

Young Tucker came over to her, leaned down, and asked, "Libby, what can I do to be of help?"

His compassion obviously had a soothing effect. Looking up at him with moist brown eyes, Libby told him in a surprisingly composed voice, "You are very kind—just like your father." Lifting her eyes to Colby, who stood over her, she added, "I don't know what I would have done without him."

The older Tucker felt his face color. "I don't know anyone who would've done otherwise, honey," he said gently. Turning to Jeff, he asked, "Son, I can understand your wanting to help out, but what about your job?"

Straightening up, Jeff assured him, "It's being taken care of. There's just no way I'm going to let you trail Malone any farther without me, Dad. We know what a madman he is."

Colby nodded and ran a finger across his mustache. "Okay, son. But before we get back on Malone's trail, we've got to find Libby a place to stay in Fort Worth. We sure can't leave her here by herself. It's a hard enough time for her to be alone, but especially not with Comanches on the prowl."

"They're more than prowling," the young lawman responded. "Early this morning I found the bodies of two men who'd been scalped—federal marshals, in fact. I had briefly met them in Waco; they were tracking Malone, too." He shook his head and added softly, "They were real eager to find him before you did."

No one spoke for a few moments, then Jeff suggested, "Libby, Dad and I will help you with . . . with your parents and your brother. Do you want to take them to Fort Worth for burial, or do you want them buried here?"

Looking shattered by her ordeal, Libby stood up and

answered wearily, "I want to bury them right here. This is our home—or at least it was."

It was early afternoon by the time the burials were completed. Colby Tucker rested on his shovel and looked down at the Daly farm from the vantage point of the hilltop, turning back to his son as Jeff declared, "Well, I guess that should do it." The younger Tucker tossed one last shovelful of dirt onto the common grave, and then Libby Malone approached, carrying a fistful of wildflowers in one hand and the family Bible in the other.

Standing between the two men, Libby opened the Bible to the Twenty-third Psalm and began to read, but she had gotten no further than the first few words when she began to weep. Jeff put a strong arm around her shoulders while Colby took the book from her hands and finished reading.

When he had completed the passage, Libby asked to have a few moments alone at the gravesite before she joined them in the buckboard to go back to the house.

"Sure thing," Colby responded. "Take your time." Putting his arm around his son, he led Jeff over by the wagon that sat underneath the spreading branches of a huge oak tree.

Leaning against the wagon, the two men stood watching Libby, who had her back to them. "You know, Son," Colby began, "that woman has more spunk and courage than I think I've ever seen in anybody."

"She sure has. I know the pain I'm feeling over losing Jim; I can only begin to imagine what she's feeling."

Colby peered intently at his son. "You seem to like her, boy. I mean, *really* like her."

Blushing slightly, Jeff replied, "Yeah, I guess I do."

There was an awkward silence between the two men for a moment, then Jeff changed the subject, telling his father, "When I got back to Waco in response to your wire, Mayor Teague asked me about becoming McLennan County's sheriff—with the voters' approval, of course."

Colby looked at his son sharply, took a breath, and asked, "What did you tell him?"

"I said if the people wanted me, I'd do it. Only it would have to wait until I found you and helped you bring in Malone. He said he'd keep the job open till I got back. By the way, Wayne Dunne seems to have things under control."

Colby Tucker's weathered face broke into a wide smile. "Jeff, nothing could make me happier. You know how proud I was to have Jim step into my boots. Well, Son, I'd be just as proud to have you do it."

"Thanks, Dad. That means a lot to me."

"Of course," the older man went on, "I can't rightly say how pleased your mother will be to have you in the exact same job as got your brother killed. . . . But the way I figure it, she's a lawman's wife, always has been. You're a lawman, too, and with you in Waco rather than Nacogdoches, she'd get to see a lot more of you."

"That's right, Dad," Jeff agreed.

Libby finally returned to the wagon, a look of resignation on her face. "I'm ready to go now," she told the two lawmen softly. Looking up at the sun, she added, "It's long past lunchtime. How about if I fix us all something to eat?"

Jeff smiled sweetly at her. "That'd be just fine. I'm mighty hungry, I confess. How about you, Dad?"

"I sure won't refuse," Colby assured her, giving her a quick, consoling hug.

An hour later Colby Tucker pushed back his empty plate and declared, "Well, I guess it's time we get going. Libby, why don't you pack whatever things you'll be needing—and figure out where you can stay in Fort Worth. Do you have any friends you can live with for a while?"

"I don't want to stay in Fort Worth. I want to go with the two of you."

Taken aback by this unexpected demand, Colby asserted, "I'm afraid that won't be possible, Libby. Chasing down your father isn't going to be an easy task. It could mean weeks of hard riding, a lot of hours a day. And when we finally catch up to him, it's going to be plenty dangerous—there's sure to be a shoot-out and bloodshed. I can't allow you to face that kind of danger."

"I've been in that kind of danger right here," she countered. Leaning forward, she gazed intently into Colby's eyes and pleaded, "Please don't make me stay behind. After what Duke did to this family, I want to see him captured. If he's going to be killed, I want to see that, too. I believe I have a right to be there when he's brought to justice."

The sadness etched on her lovely face tore at Colby Tucker's heart, but he knew he was right.

"Please," she repeated, looking from one man to the other, "please take me with you."

Reaching for her hand, Jeff told her tenderly, "Listen to me. Everything is going to be all right. I know the whole world looks black to you right now, but you're young, bright, and . . . and very beautiful. You've got a happy future ahead. I promise."

Colby caught his son's eyes across the table, and he could see that his son was wavering. Jeff was attracted to Libby; it was written all over him. Holding Jeff's pale-blue eyes with his own, Colby told the young lawman sternly, "She'd slow us down, and it's simply too dangerous. We'll find her a place to stay in Fort Worth and then be on our way."

Stubbornly sticking out her chin, Libby declared, "Sheriff Tucker, I'm most appreciative for all the help you've given me, but the fact is, I don't have to take your advice."

Colby stared at her for a long moment. Then, shaking

his head, he said, "Little gal, you have a way of talking without using words. Let me see if I'm getting your message. Are you telling me that if I refuse to let you ride with us, you'll get aboard a horse and follow us anyway?"

A wry smile curved Libby's mouth. "Sheriff Tucker," she replied, tilting her pretty head, "you got my message perfectly. I practically grew up on a horse, and I can ride as far and as fast as any man."

Jeff tried to stifle a laugh, but he did not succeed.

Colby could not make up his mind whether to be annoyed or amused. He finally chose the latter. Throwing up his hands in mock anguish, he declared, "Okay, I surrender." Then growing serious, he told Libby, "But I want you to tell me if you change your mind. We're going to be setting a tough pace, and I don't want you thinking you have to go on if at any time you feel you can't. We can always take you to the nearest town, where you can wait for us to return for you. Is it a deal?"

Libby Malone threw her arms around his neck. "It's a deal," she promised.

Colby stood up from the table, "Okay, kids. Let's get at it."

Chapter Nine

The sun had been below the horizon for almost a half hour when Duke Malone and his two cohorts crested a hill and the town of Decatur came into view.

Tired and thirsty, George Niles lifted his hat and ran a dusty sleeve across his brow. "Whew, am I glad we're staying in Decatur tonight," he sighed. "A nice soft hotel bed is gonna feel mighty good to these poor aching bones."

"After we leave Decatur," Harry Blevins asked, "how much longer d'you figure we'll have to ride to get to where we're going?"

Malone flicked his smoking stub of a cigarette to the ground and replied, "As long as it takes, friend. Why? You gettin' tired and want to quit? Losin' interest in bein' rich?"

"No, no, Duke," Blevins protested. "I only meant I'm getting bone-weary, like George here. We'll both be fine after we rest up."

"That's good," Malone replied, " 'cause we've got some ridin' to do yet. The money's stashed east of Roland, on the Red River. But don't worry. There ain't no sense in killin' ourselves, and we gotta think of the horses, too. 'Sides which, I want to time it so's we get there durin' daylight. We have to be able to see to dig for the money." Malone spurred his mount forward. "Now let's get goin' and find us some chow in town."

*   *   *

Decatur, Texas, like dozens of other towns on the raw frontier, consisted of one main street roughly three blocks long. Lining both sides of the dusty thoroughfare was a ragtag line of buildings of various sizes and heights, some with porch overhangs, some without. Most of the false-fronted buildings were framed timber; a few were of stucco. All were worn and sun bleached.

The light was deepening from faded orange to purple as the three fugitives rode into town. George Niles watched the few people walking along the boardwalks, most of them coming out of business establishments that were closing for the day. With an inward sigh he thought how untroubled they all looked. If it were not for the fact that he desperately needed his share of the money, he would have slipped away from Duke Malone days before. But he had burned his bridges behind him and was a wanted man now, and he needed the money to live on when he crossed the border into Mexico.

"You told us you've been here before," Blevins suddenly said to Malone. "How many saloons has this town got?"

"Four," came the rapid reply. "My favorite one's right across the street from the hotel."

At the far corner of the second block Malone guided his horse to the hitch rail in front of the North Star Hotel. Blevins and Niles drew up beside him and looked across the street at the saloon. "The Gunslinger," Blevins read the sign aloud, dismounting. "Wonder why anybody would put a name like that on a saloon?"

Malone swung down from his saddle. Pulling a ready-made cigarette from a shirt pocket, he stuck it between his lips. Before lighting up, he asked Blevins, "You ever hear of Monty Whalen?"

"Yeah. He was a gunfighter. One of the best. Never did know what happened to him."

"He used to own that saloon," Malone informed him,

flaring the match on the hitch rail. He lit the cigarette and took a long pull before throwing the match to the ground. Exhaling a cloud of smoke, he continued, "At the peak of his gunfightin' powers, Whalen took a fall off his horse and broke both his shoulders real bad. It happened not too far from here. He couldn't draw his guns again, so he took up gamblin'."

Blevins chuckled. "You're not going to tell me Whalen won that saloon in a poker game."

"Exactly," Malone assured him. "He took the owner of the saloon on in a game and beat him, and in honor of his old profession, he changed the name of the place to the Gunslinger. It sort of attracted travelers, so the new owner left the name when he took over."

"What happened to Whalen?" queried Niles.

Malone chortled. "A gunfighter by the name of Jack Box had it in for Monty. Seems Monty's woman had once been Box's girl. Took Box a while to find 'em, but when he did, he blasted 'em both into eternity."

Niles shrugged his shoulders, chuckling, "That's the way it goes, I guess—you win some and you lose some. But what the hell. I don't really give a damn what happened to some guy I never met. Are we gonna get us a drink first or check into the hotel?"

"Neither. Let's go chow down—then we'll wet our whistles," replied Malone.

As they started along the boardwalk toward the nearest café, George Niles asked softly, "Duke, why do you suppose we haven't been attacked by any federal men yet? Doesn't that seem kind of strange?"

"Guess they're too stupid to find us," Malone replied drily.

"They'd have to be awful damn stupid in that case, 'cause we've let our faces be seen a lot more than we'd planned to in the first place."

Hitching up his gun belt, Malone declared, "Maybe they're just too scared to go up against me. Maybe they trailed us for a while, then tucked their tails between their legs and went back to Austin, tellin' their head man that they just couldn't find us. Or maybe them Comanches scared 'em off." He gave an explosive bark of laughter, declaring, "Fact is, I don't rightly care why we ain't seen hide nor hair of 'em—it just saves me the trouble of havin' to kill 'em, is all."

After their meal Malone, Niles, and Blevins sauntered back along the street. Niles suggested they should check into the hotel and put their horses in a stable for the night, but Malone said he wanted a drink first, so they crossed over to the Gunslinger Saloon.

When they pushed their way through the batwing doors, the loud banging on the upright piano and the raucous laughter became almost deafening. Leading the way, Malone swaggered into the barroom that smelled of heavy smoke, sweat, and stale whiskey.

The killer threaded his way among the tables until he reached an empty one alongside the far wall. As he sat down, Malone waved a hand at the bartender and shouted above the din, "Whiskey!"

Just as Niles and Blevins reached the table, two drifters carrying glasses and bottles suddenly shouted, "Hey! That's our table!" and rushed over.

Niles and Blevins slowly, almost disinterestedly, turned to face them. But Malone immediately grew angry, and he stood up so fast that he knocked his chair over backward. His cold black eyes were belligerent, and looking hard at the drifter closer to him, he demanded, "What's your name?"

"Fred Tudor. What's it to you?"

Ignoring the question, Malone looked past him and asked the other one, "What's yours?"

"Clete Bain. And like my friend said, why do you wanna know?"

Malone leaned over the table and scanned its top.

Then slowly rising to his full height, he glared at each of them and growled, "Well, now, gents, fact is, I don't see either of your names carved on this table you claim is yours—but maybe I'm overlookin' the spot. Why don't you point it out to me?"

By this time the noise in the saloon had subsided, the piano had stopped, and everyone stared at the five men, waiting. The bartender in particular—a beefy, bald-headed man with a droopy handlebar mustache—was watching the confrontation intently from behind the bar.

"We was sittin' here before we went to get our drinks," the man named Bain declared, "so this is our table."

Malone looked at Bain with surprise. "You mean a man don't even get his drinks delivered to him in this crummy joint?"

"That's the way it is," the bartender confirmed from across the room.

"Oh, yeah?" Malone taunted. "And does the owner of this here barroom know he's got one lazy bastard workin' for him?"

The bartender sneered at the killer. "I'd say so. You see, I'm the owner."

"Hah!" the drifter named Tudor cackled into Malone's face. "I guess you'll have to go to the bar to get your drinks after all, mister—and while you and your friends are doin' that, me and Clete will take *our* table."

Malone's face distorted with rage. Without warning he jerked the bottle and glass from Tudor's hands, snapping, "Looks like I've got my drink right here!"

Lunging at Malone, Tudor bared his teeth and growled, "Why you—"

The killer smashed the bottle down so savagely on Tudor's head that it shattered, showering the man with glass and whiskey. As Tudor fell stunned, Clete Bain dropped his glass and bottle and clawed for his sidearm. Before it cleared its holster, the drifter was looking into the ominous black bore of Duke Malone's right-hand gun. Obviously expecting the gun to roar and blow his head off, Bain shook with terror.

"Maybe you'd like to say a little prayer before I pump some lead into your throat," Malone snarled. "Lead's mighty hard to digest—and you might just die tryin' to swallow it."

Suddenly the bartender's deep voice thundered across the room. "You ain't killing nobody in here, you damn buzzard!" Backing up his words was a double-barreled twelve-gauge shotgun with both hammers thumbed back, ready to fire.

Everyone standing or sitting between the bar and Duke Malone scattered, clearing a path between them.

George Niles put a nervous hand on the killer's arm. "Come on, Duke," he said in a placating voice. "Let it go. We can have a drink somewhere else—after all, you said there are four saloons in this town."

Malone did not move a muscle.

"Put the gun in its holster and get your carcass out of here, you buzzard!" blared the bartender. *"Now!"* There was no doubt, from the look on the man's face, that he meant business.

The saloon was as quiet as a tomb at midnight. Niles feared he knew Mad Dog Malone all too well—and that meant the killer would not let matters go and just walk away. But then Malone surprised him, and in a deliberate, cautious move, he eased down the revolver's hammer and dropped the gun into its holster.

Holding his hands waist-high, he spread them in a placating gesture and, gazing steadily at the barkeep, walked toward the bar and offered, "Now, mister, I didn't come in here to cause no trouble. Any of these fine gentlemen seated near this table will testify that my friends and I chose it 'cause no one was sittin' here. We was rudely approached by these two ruffians, who seem to think they own this table."

The bartender watched his progress warily.

"All my friends and I wanted when we came in here was to relax and have a few drinks. We don't want no trouble. If you was watchin', you saw that guy go for his weapon first. Was I supposed to just stand there and let him shoot me?"

As Malone inched his way closer to him, the bartender seemed mesmerized by his mild words. "Well, no," the saloon owner admitted. "But you busted his friend pretty good with that bottle." He gestured with his chin at the now-seated Fred Tudor dabbing at a cut on his head with a dirty bandanna.

George Niles and Harry Blevins stood as still as statues, not even daring to look at each other. They knew what was coming as sure as Monday follows Sunday.

Stepping still closer, Malone responded, "Yep, I did use the bottle. Let me ask you, though: Did you see how fast I drew my gun?"

"Yeah."

"Then I *could* have shot him dead instead of hittin' him with the bottle, couldn't I?"

"Yeah."

"So you see," Malone said persuasively as he approached within inches of the bar, "I weren't nearly as nasty as I could've been."

Apparently lulled by Malone's tone, the bartender was off his guard. Suddenly, before the barkeep even had time to react, Malone seized the shotgun by the barrels and ripped it from his hands. The killer held the weapon in his right hand while with his left he grabbed the bartender's shirt and yanked him over the bar. Flattening him on the floor, Malone rammed the muzzles of the shotgun into the bartender's mouth, breaking off several of his teeth.

The saloon owner lay sweating with terror, gagging as Malone pushed the muzzles farther into his mouth. His chest rose and fell in quick pants, and his whole body trembled like a quaking aspen in a storm. Taunting him, Malone hissed, "One way I'd never want to die is by shotgun. Leaves one hell of a mess for the next of kin, don't you agree?"

George Niles felt the bile rising in his stomach yet again. No matter how long he rode with Duke Malone, the man's behavior did not get any easier to bear—nor did it become any less sadistic. Malone was clearly enjoying the bartender's terror. He stood there jeering at the man, laughing wickedly, and the evil glint in Malone's eyes made Niles want to scream at him and demand that he stop acting like a madman . . . except that he did not dare. Still, he had to do something. Swallowing against his rising gorge, George Niles had seen all he could stand. He dashed across the room and pleaded with the killer, "Duke, don't do this! There's no need to kill the man!"

Not moving his eyes from his victim, Malone's lip curled back and he snarled at Niles, "I'm sick of your soft attitude, George. A fella can't run with me and wear lace underwear. You need to toughen up—like me."

The sudden roar of the shotgun made everybody in the room jerk reflexively as the bartender's head was blown apart. Wild-eyed, Duke Malone stared at each person in the saloon as if daring them to make a move, and they all stood staring back, paralyzed with shock and fear.

Then came rapid footsteps on the boardwalk outside. Malone swung the shotgun toward the door, his finger poised on the second trigger. A glint of the badge on the marshal's chest as he burst through the batwings, gun drawn, was all anyone got to see, for at the same instant Mad Dog Malone let go with the other barrel. Taking the lethal impact full in the chest, Decatur's town marshal was slammed across the boardwalk, landing half in the street.

Throwing down the empty shotgun, Malone whipped out both revolvers and waved them at the crowd in the saloon. "Anybody who moves a muscle dies!" With a toss of his head he ordered his partners, "Let's go!"

While Blevins and Niles circled around him, Malone growled at the saloon patrons, "If any of you is thinkin' about followin' after us, you better forget it. I guarantee you'll die if you do."

Malone quickly backed out of the batwing doors and ran across the street to his horse on the heels of his companions. As they untied their mounts and leaped into their saddles, George Niles told himself mockingly, "And to think I actually believed I could sleep in a real bed tonight."

Sheriff Colby Tucker's years of experience immediately put him back onto Mad Dog Malone's trail. The killer had returned to Fort Worth, rejoined his partners, then headed north. From time to time Colby's second guessing was confirmed by someone who had seen three men heading in the direction of Wichita Falls, and the description given of the man who seemed to be in charge fit Malone perfectly.

By early afternoon on the second day of travel, the two Tucker men and Libby Malone were within some fifteen miles of Decatur. Halting beside a stream, the threesome ate a leisurely meal, then watered the animals. Jeff and Libby knelt on the stream bank to fill their canteens, obviously enjoying each other's company. The older Tucker tightened the cinch on his saddle and surreptitiously watched his son and Libby, but they seemed to be completely unaware of him. He smiled, thinking how resilient young people were. In the midst of terrible tragedy life went on and new bonds were formed. Indeed, perhaps it was *because* of their sharing in tragedy that Libby and Jeff were drawn to each other, looking for new hope and strength. Colby sighed and patted his horse's long neck, wishing that he could lay aside his torment as easily—but he could not. It was eating at him like gangrene, and the only thing that would put it to rest was the capture—and death—of Mad Dog Duke Malone.

He automatically checked the loads in his revolver again, then took out his derringer to check it as well. He might well need it before this manhunt was over.

Jeff and Libby strolled up from the creek with the canteens just as Colby was about to slip the derringer back into its pouch. The glinting metal caught the young woman's eye, and when she saw what it was, she asked in a surprised voice, "You carry a derringer on you, Sheriff?"

"Whenever I'm wearing my gun belt," he confirmed with a nod. Turning the belt inside out, he displayed the pouch sewn near the end of the belt, close to the buckle. "See that?"

"Uh-huh."

"I had it stitched in there so I could carry the derringer without its being noticed. Never hurts for a fella to have a little something to back him up in case he needs it."

"Derringers are so small," observed the blonde. "I've often wondered if they're powerful enough to kill a man."

Tilting the gun so she could see the twin vertical bores, he advised, "Take a look at the size of those barrels. Forty-one caliber, honey. Yeah, it's powerful enough, all right—although it has to be within close range to be accurate. Best thing about it is that it gives you an edge. Your adversary usually doesn't know you're carrying it."

Libby giggled. "Especially if it's as well concealed as yours."

Colby smiled. "That's the whole point." He put the weapon back into its pouch, then looked up at the sky. "Well, time's a-passing. We'd best get back in the saddle. I think we're gaining ground on Malone and his cronies, and I don't want to lag behind."

They mounted up, and as they rode on, Jeff queried, "Dad, you're certain that Malone's heading for Wichita Falls?"

"Yep. I'm pretty sure Malone is out to get Hans Brummer, and since he no doubt remembers that Hans has a brother living there, what better way to find out where Hans is now?"

"He won't have far to look once he's found Hans's brother, that's for sure."

"Nope—apparently they live within blocks of each other. If Malone gets to Wichita Falls, there's no doubt in my mind that Hans is a dead man. I'm just hoping we can catch up with him before he gets there."

"I think there's another reason Duke Malone is headed north, Sheriff," Libby said, so softly that Colby almost did not hear her.

"What's that?" the sheriff asked.

"I remember him coming to the house on the way to his hideout just before you trapped him and arrested him. He had just robbed that bank, and he bragged to my mother that he had buried the money somewhere on the banks of the Red River. My guess is that it's still there."

Colby looked thoughtful as he stroked his mustache. "I see. In that case there's a possibility he'd head for his money, then go after Hans. Since we don't know where the loot is hidden, we'll just have to head for Wichita Falls. Well, at any rate, we'll stay in Decatur tonight and get a good early start in the morning. We've got to catch Malone before he gets the chance to kill again."

Dusk found the trio entering Decatur weary and ready for a night's rest. They did not even have to ask if Duke Malone and his two companions had been there. Everyone in town was talking about the vicious, ugly man who had blown the saloon owner's head off with his own shotgun.

They took rooms at the North Star Hotel and had dinner in the small restaurant downstairs, called the Wagon Wheel Café. Immediately after eating, the Tuckers and Libby Malone approached the desk clerk and requested that hot water be brought up for bathing. That done, the threesome wearily climbed the stairs to the second floor, Colby and Jeff opening the door to room six and Libby going into the adjoining room.

Colby had insisted that Jeff bathe first, and after the young man had done so, clean hot water was delivered for the older man's bath. While his father settled in the wooden tub, enjoying the soothing warmth, Jeff climbed back into his clothes.

"Hey, boy! What're you doing?" Colby wondered.

"Going next door for a few minutes," Jeff answered. "I want to make sure Libby is all right."

Colby eyed him with speculation. "I'm sure if she wasn't, she'd holler. Walls aren't so thick that we wouldn't hear her."

"I won't be long," Jeff assured him, and disappeared through the door.

Strolling the few steps along the corridor to the next room, the tall, handsome young lawman tapped on Libby's door. Light footsteps were heard, then she called through the door, "Yes?"

"It's Jeff," he called.

"I'll be right there."

The door opened a few moments later, and Libby stood shyly with the bedspread wrapped around her like an oversize shawl. There was a shine on her face and a warm smile on her lips, and she smelled wonderfully of lavender-scented soap from her recent bath.

"I hope I'm not intruding. I, uh, just wanted to check on you before I turned in for the night," he told her, drinking in her beauty.

"You're not intruding at all, and I'm fine," she replied, her hand holding on to the door, "thanks to you and your father."

"Good," he responded, a somewhat foolish grin on his face. "Well, I'll see you in the morning." With that he turned and started to leave.

"Jeff . . ."

Halting in midstep, he turned back to face her. "Yes, Libby?"

"Thank you for being so kind to me."

He blushed, suddenly feeling shy and awkward, and ran his fingers through his thick, dark hair. "It's . . . my pleasure. My dad's tried to teach me to be a gentleman."

Letting go of the door, Libby stepped closer to him. The overwhelming scent of lavender stirred him, and he felt his heart drumming against his ribs.

"He's done a good job," she said softly.

Jeff Tucker found it hard to breathe. Libby Malone was the most beautiful woman he had ever seen, but as much as he wanted to say so, he could not bring himself to do it. Instead he said, "Libby, I . . . I wanted to tell you that I never met a girl like you before." He swallowed, then added, "I just want you to know that I think you're incredible—uh, that is, I mean how you're managing so well with everything that's happened to you, and keeping up so well on this journey and all. . . ."

Jeff watched her lips as they curved into a sweet smile, and he hungered to kiss them.

"I think you're very special, too, Jeff."

An awkward silence fell between them. The young marshal wanted to take her in his arms so badly that he trembled. The silence lingered for a few more seconds, then he broke it by taking a deep breath and saying, "Well, I guess I'd better hit the hay. See you in the morning."

"See you in the morning," she echoed.

Hurrying to his room, the tall young man looked back to see Libby watching him. She smiled warmly at him, and he smiled in return, then entered the room.

Colby was sitting on the bed in his long underwear, drying his hair with a towel. As Jeff began unbuttoning his shirt, the elder Tucker warned, "Better go slow, Son."

"Huh? What are you talking about?"

"Libby. Don't let your heart get in the way of good sense and run away with you."

Removing the shirt from his muscular body, Jeff said, "You've got to admit she's one sweet girl, Dad. And awfully beautiful."

"That she is, Son," the elder lawman admitted, grinning. "Next to your mother, I guess she's about the prettiest woman I've ever laid eyes on." He grew serious, saying, "I'm not trying to butt into your business, or run your life—hell, you're a big boy now. It's just that Libby's been through so much . . . and for that matter, so have you. These kinds of troubles . . . Well, I guess what I'm trying to say is that when you settle down to one woman, you need the proper foundation. For your own sake, and for hers, just go slow, okay?"

"Sure, Dad. And I appreciate your concern for both of us."

The lamp was doused and the two men climbed into bed. In the dark silence Jeff thought about the beautiful woman in the next room, wishing he had taken her in his arms and kissed her.

The Wagon Wheel Café opened for business at the crack of dawn, and Colby and Jeff Tucker and Libby Malone were among the first to arrive for breakfast. Other patrons followed, either singly or in small groups, and soon the restaurant was filled with the clatter of dishes and the voices of the diners.

The threesome had just finished eating when four

men sat down next to their table and began talking excitedly among themselves. Colby picked up the word "massacre," and turning to them, he inquired, "Pardon me, gentlemen, I'm Sheriff Colby Tucker from McLennan County. Did I hear someone say there's been a massacre?"

"That's right, Sheriff," one of the men in the group informed him. "We just came down from the north, and we heard about a Comanche war party that massacred two families on neighborin' farms. They were all killed and scalped—even five little children. Happened late yesterday afternoon about twenty miles or so from here."

"They say it's the work of that chieftain Bald Eagle," put in another in the group.

Colby's ears perked up. "Bald Eagle? You're sure?"

"Yeah."

"Thank you for the information, sir," Colby responded. He turned back to his table and stared down at his plate, shaking his head.

"Do you suppose he's the same one, Dad?" Jeff asked, surprise evident on his face.

Libby seemed bewildered. "What are you talking about?" she asked, looking from one Tucker to the other.

"I saved Bald Eagle's life years ago, and to show his gratitude, he said for the rest of his life I would be his white brother."

"Is that a fact!" the young woman exclaimed. "How did that happen?"

Colby's eyes looked faraway as he recalled the events. "It happened back in the winter of sixty-three. For almost ten years there had been peace between whites and Comanches in our part of Texas. The Comanches had established a large village a few miles outside of Waco, and their chief—a fellow by the name of White Fang—well, he and I were pretty friendly. He had a young son who was called Little Sparrow, and one cold day I stopped by the village to powwow with White Fang and found that Little Sparrow was deathly sick with a high fever."

"How old was Little Sparrow then?" queried Libby.

"He was—well, let's see . . . uh . . . about nine, I'd guess," replied Colby. "Yeah, nine; about a year older than Jeff was. Anyway, the Comanche medicine man had been unable to help Little Sparrow, so I told White Fang we should get him into town to the doctor. The chief and his squaw showed some fear at that suggestion, and the medicine man didn't like it at all. They're pesky critters, those medicine men; they hold a lot of religious power over their people. I could see the boy was in bad shape and would probably die if he didn't get some proper doctoring, and I said so to White Fang. The medicine man, who was standing right there, was madder than a wet hen." Colby chuckled. "Actually, he threatened to put an arrow between my shoulder blades if I tried to take the boy from the village."

"So what did you do?" Libby asked, caught up in the tale.

Colby shifted in his chair and took a sip of his coffee before replying. "I took a chance. I could see that even though White Fang was the chief, he was afraid to cross the medicine man—but on the other hand, I couldn't let the little guy die. So I picked the boy up and carried him to my horse—all the time expecting to get an arrow in the back. But it never came. When I was settled in the saddle with the child in my arms, I told White Fang and his squaw that I would take Little Sparrow to my house, and I would have him examined by the doctor as soon as he could ride out there. They agreed to this, and then they hopped on their pintos and traveled with me. As it turned out, Little Sparrow had scarlet fever. The doc said he would have died in a few more hours if I hadn't brought him in."

Libby cocked her head. "And this Little Sparrow is . . . Bald Eagle?"

"Yep," Colby confirmed, nodding. "The scarlet fever burned out the roots of his hair. When it all fell out and never grew back, his parents renamed him."

"So he really *is* bald?"

"Like a Texas rock." Colby took another sip of coffee and said, "The little guy stayed at our house for quite some time, until he was fully recovered. Edie and the boys grew to love him."

"There was certainly nothing savage about him then," put in Jeff, smiling. "I remember how much I liked him. Heck, we had a great time playing together after he got better."

Colby laughed. "I remember. When it came time for you to do your chores, you were nowhere to be found." He sighed, adding, "When White Fang came to take his son back to the village, the little guy put his arms around me and thanked me for saving his life. Said we would be brothers forever. Not too long after that there was war between our two peoples again, and Chief White Fang was killed in a battle."

"When was the last time you saw Bald Eagle, Dad?" asked Jeff.

The lawman thought a few seconds then replied, "It must be ten years now, 'cause he was about sixteen at the time. He renewed his pledge that we would be brothers forever. I heard he became a chief about three years ago." Colby stared at his empty plate, his mind preoccupied. "I guess he's changed a whole lot," he finally murmured. "I sure hope that if we run into him, he won't have changed so much that he doesn't remember me—or the bond we have."

Chapter Ten

It was midmorning the next day when Libby Malone and the Tuckers rode into the small town of Henrietta, Texas, finding it almost deserted. Looking up and down the length of the main street, Colby remarked to his companions, "Looks like there's only one saloon to check out. No hotel that I can see. That makes it easy for us to find out if the mad dog and his two hounds have been here. If so, it'll confirm they're headed for Wichita Falls."

The three of them dismounted, and Jeff advised the young woman, "You wait here with the horses, Libby. Dad and I will be right back."

"All right, Jeff," she agreed, wrapping her reins around the hitch rail. She watched the two men—Jeff in particular—until they disappeared into the dark interior of the Old Corral Saloon. Smiling to herself, she turned back around and found herself looking into the faces of two young, husky men who were obviously saddletramps. They were dirty and unshaven and smelled of sweat and horses.

"Howdy, girlie," said the taller one, grinning, exposing a mouthful of filthy yellow teeth. "You're sure a purty little thing—ain't she, Julius?"

"I'll say, Avery. And it seems like she ain't got nothin' to do . . . so what say we entertain her?"

Libby eyed them coldly, feeling complete repugnance. Lifting her graceful chin, she pointedly turned away.

The man named Avery took hold of her arm and spun her around. "Hey, honey, don't you be stuck up now."

Her brown eyes flashed with anger, and Libby jerked her arm free and spat, "You get away from me!"

The man seized her arm again and pulled her close. She struggled, but she could not break loose from his powerful grip. "I told you to get away from me!" she squealed. "Leave me alone!"

He just laughed and drew her closer. His foul breath was repulsive as he declared, "Now, girlie, you don't mean that. When a woman tells a handsome fella like me to leave her alone, I know what she really means. She really means the opposite. Now, ain't that so?"

He wrapped his arms around her and bent his head down to kiss her, but Libby jerked her face away and pushed with all her might against him. A bit off balance, he released her enough to steady himself, and when he did so, Libby worked her hands free and slapped him across the face as hard as she could.

"Get your filthy paws off her!" Jeff Tucker's voice suddenly roared from across the street.

Libby looked over at the saloon, feeling greatly relieved.

Slamming through the swinging doors of the saloon with his father two steps behind, the young marshal, his face red with rage, bounded toward the two saddle-tramps. "If you're smart, mister, you'll let go of the young lady immediately," Jeff warned.

Avery turned his head to look at his challenger, then released Libby and stood defensively. After peering at the badge on the young man's chest, the drifter looked insolently at him and said, "That there tin star says Nacogdoches. This ain't Nacogdoches, lawman. You ain't got no jurisdiction here. Looks like I got as much right to court the lady as anyone."

Jeff stepped closer, and when he was near enough, the drifter abruptly swung at him, but the younger man easily dodged the big balled fist and countered with a blow that sent the saddletramp sprawling onto the dusty street. Libby quickly backed away, heading for the senior Tucker nearby.

Suddenly the other drifter leaped into the fray, swearing loudly. But as marshal of a tough Texas town, Jeff was no stranger to a street brawl, and he clamped the man's shoulders with both hands and threw him to the ground. The man wheezed as his breath was knocked out of him, and then he moaned loudly.

"Jeff, look out!" Libby yelled.

Young Tucker turned to find Avery coming at him, the man's eyes brimming with rage. Jeff stopped him with a punch on the nose, then followed it up with a left and a right to the jaw. Furious and undaunted, the husky saddletramp charged his slimmer opponent again, but the marshal sidestepped the man, who collided instead with the rump of Jeff's horse. The startled animal whinnied, dancing out of the way, and the man fell to his knees.

"Sheriff Tucker, can't you do something?" Libby asked fearfully.

Shaking his head, Colby replied, "I don't think my son would want me to interfere, my dear. A man needs to fight his own battles, after all." Patting Libby's shoulder, he added, "Don't you worry none. I've seen Jeff take a lot worse—and with very little wear and tear. The boy's damn tough, I promise."

As Avery struggled to his feet, his cohort started toward Jeff, snarling. But Colby Tucker planted himself in front of the man. "I'll have to draw the line here, mister," he warned. "Let's keep the odds nice and even. You stay out of it."

The hefty saddletramp eyed the older lawman, looking him up and down arrogantly, then sneered. "Your badge says you're sheriff of McLennan County," he grunted. "That means you ain't got jurisdiction here no more'n the marshal. You'd better get your carcass out of my way, or you're gonna get hurt, old man. Now, move it!"

The strapping lawman merely stared at the drifter. "Why don't you make me move, big mouth?"

Swearing, the man named Julius went after him. Adeptly the lawman grasped the saddletramp's right wrist, spinning him around and giving his arm a savage twist. A bone snapped loudly in the man's shoulder, and he howled in agony. "I'll kill you!" he screamed, clawing at the gun on his right hip with his left hand.

But Colby grabbed the revolver and heaved it onto the porch overhang of the building behind them. Grabbing the man by the other arm, Colby hissed, "I'll break this one too, mister, if you try anything else— that's a promise!"

It was all too evident that the sheriff was not making an idle threat. Holding his injured arm, the man sheepishly backed away, watching helplessly as his friend and the young lawman tangled.

The fight was all over in a matter of seconds. Jeff Tucker landed one last solid haymaker to the drifter's face, knocking him out cold. Dashing to her defender, Libby exclaimed, "Oh, Jeff, are you all right?"

"Sure," he assured her, panting and smiling through a split lip.

"But your face is bleeding and your lip is cut."

"Nothing that a little time won't heal," he gasped, trying to catch his breath. "I'll be fine."

"There's a water trough over there in front of the tobacco shop." She pointed diagonally across the street. "Come, let me wash you up." Looking over her shoulder at Colby, Libby asked, "Sheriff? Are you coming?"

Colby shook his head and smiled. "You two go on. I

see that an old friend of mine is finally coming to the rescue."

Looking to where the sheriff was gesturing, Libby saw the town marshal elbowing his way through the crowd that had formed. "Well, all right," she said to Colby as the other lawman came toward them, "in that case I'll take care of your son."

"I've no doubt you will," Colby murmured, his eyes twinkling.

Blushing slightly, Libby took Jeff's arm. As she started to leave, the two old lawmen loudly greeted each other.

"Colby Tucker!" the town marshal declared. "What in tarnation are you doing here? You always did show up at the oddest times."

"And I might tell you the same thing, Barry Wheaton," Colby replied. "And just what brought you here to Henrietta? Last I knew, you were still marshal down at Corpus Christi."

"I was, up until a year ago, but my wife missed her kinfolk. Tell me, did you see what happened here?"

Colby scratched his nose. "Well, yeah. Actually, I was . . . uh . . . sort of part of it."

Libby and Jeff flicked each other an amused glance, and then they left the two old lawmen to reminisce with each other. She guided him to the water trough; then, kneeling in front of it, she said, "Let me have your bandanna, Jeff." Libby studied Jeff's battered face while he pulled the red and white dotted bandanna from his hip pocket, then shook her head, saying softly, "I'm so sorry for causing this."

"You didn't cause it, Libby," he assured her tenderly.

"But if I hadn't been riding with you—"

"Hush, now, and clean up my ugly mug. We're going to need to get moving. Dad and I learned in the saloon that Duke and his companions were here in town late yesterday. They stayed a few hours—one of their horses needed a new shoe, and they whiled away the time in the saloon. Someone overheard them talking about camping north of town."

Libby gasped. "Really? Then we *are* gaining on them!"

"Yeah. But you can be sure they left this morning, so we need to pull out as fast as we can."

Libby plunged the bandanna into the cool water, wrung it out, and dabbed at Jeff's cuts and bruises. He winced when the wet cloth first touched his face. "Oh! Sorry," she whispered. "I'll be as gentle as I can."

Jeff leaned toward her. "You're doing fine," he told her, his voice husky.

Libby blushed again and turned away to rinse the cloth, trying to hide the unsettling feelings rising within her.

"Libby? . . ."

"Hmm?"

"I've been wanting to say something to you."

She turned toward him again, her heart beating fast. "Yes?"

He stared at her for a moment as if suddenly stricken dumb. "I, uh . . . well . . . I just want to say that I apologize if I embarrassed you by fighting with that scoundrel. It's just that . . . well, the thought of another man touching you is more than I can bear."

For a moment Libby saw nothing else but Jeff's handsome face. It was as if the rest of the world had slipped into a giant hole and was swallowed up, leaving just the two of them. "Oh, Jeff," she breathed. "There's nothing to apologize for. I'm not the least bit embarrassed—far from it. I feel proud and honored that you'd risk danger for me like that."

He took her hand in his. "What else could I do? I think I'm falling in love with you."

Libby's heart pounded so loudly, she was sure Jeff must have heard it. "Well, they say confession's good for the soul, so I may as well confess myself: I think I'm falling in love with *you*." She smiled, adding, "I'd kiss you to prove it if your lip wasn't cut—but I don't want to hurt you."

Jeff grinned. "Oh, I think I can stand the pain. Besides, something as sweet as a kiss from you would probably heal me instantly."

Giggling, Libby looked around. Seeing that no one was watching them, she whispered, "Maybe we should find out." Holding his face in her hands, the young blonde drew him to her and kissed him, first briefly, then lingeringly. When they separated, she sighed happily. Then, without another word, they stood up and walked back to where Colby Tucker was still talking animatedly with Marshal Barry Wheaton.

Colby turned at their approach, saying, "Well, we'd better hightail it out of here if we want to keep closing in on Malone and his cohorts. Marshal Wheaton here confirms that they were here yesterday. And a rancher coming into town this morning told Barry he'd seen smoke from a campfire off the road north of here. Probably our boys. Seems like they're in no particular hurry—I guess they're feeling mighty confident that they're free and clear, since the federal marshals didn't find them. And that means maybe we'll have the element of surprise in our favor."

Swinging into her saddle, Libby said, "I sure hope so. He may be my real father, but I want nothing more than to see him hang for what he's done."

After riding their horses at a hard gallop for some distance, Colby Tucker and his two young companions eased up and held their mounts at a steady trot. They were finally nearing Wichita Falls. About ten miles southeast of that thriving town they came upon a sparkling river lined with cottonwood trees and heavy brush.

"What river is this?" asked Libby Malone.

"The Little Wichita," came Colby's answer. "It flows into the Red River farther to the northeast." Reining his horse toward the river, the sheriff told Libby and Jeff, "We'll give the animals a short breather and let them take a drink. Then we'll have to push them hard. We've got to catch up to Malone before he gets to Wichita Falls."

"I don't see how we can be very far behind them," put in Jeff, "unless they've been riding at a hard gallop, too."

"I doubt that," said the elder Tucker. "Malone and his pals don't know we're following them, so there's no reason for them to push their horses so hard. I'm sure he's eager to find out where Hans Brummer's living, but I doubt he'd wear out his horse to do so. We ought to be seeing them up ahead of us anytime now."

Sunlight was dancing on the rippling waters of the Little Wichita as the trio guided their horses down the sloping bank to the middle of the stream. The water came almost up to their stirrups. While the horses drank, Colby looked up and down the river. Jeff and Libby had halted a few feet behind Colby, and the elder lawman heard the two of them speaking softly to each other, although he deliberately did not strain to hear what they were saying. He knew from the way they had been staring at each other the past few days that they were falling in love, and he worried that it was all happening too fast. Still, he decided to keep his peace. After all, Jeff was a grown man, and Libby seemed to be a mighty strong young woman. Smiling to himself, he had to admit that it would not displease him at all if the two of them decided to marry.

Such pleasant thoughts were suddenly interrupted when, from out of the heavy brush lining both banks of the river, rode a band of Indians. Colby spotted them a few seconds before Libby and Jeff did, and keeping his voice steady and even, he advised, "Stay calm. Don't make any sudden moves."

A tiny whimper escaped from Libby's throat, and Jeff

whispered, "It'll be all right, Libby. Dad knows how to handle Comanches."

Colby hoped his son was right. There were a dozen Indians in all surrounding them, six sitting on their ponies on the south bank, and six on the north. Their nearly naked bodies were striped with various colors of war paint, and across their foreheads and their noses from cheekbone to cheekbone were horizontal lines of yellow.

One of the Indians on the north bank lifted a hand and motioned for the trio to come his way. Colby waited for Jeff and Libby to draw alongside him before he obeyed. As they rode slowly in that direction, the six Comanche warriors on the south side rode their horses into the water and moved in behind them. From out of the corner of his eye the sheriff could see that Libby's entire body was trembling.

The Comanche who had motioned to them stared at Libby, and then a lecherous grin curled his lips, and when the trio rode up onto the riverbank, the leader spoke to his warriors in his own language. Colby Tucker knew Comanche, and he bristled at what he heard. The leader declared that they would kill the two men, and he would take the woman with the sunshine hair for himself.

As the Indians made a tight circle around them, Colby held his voice steady and said to the leader in Comanche, "You must not kill me, or my son."

The leader's eyebrows rose. "You know my tongue, old one. Then tell me why we should not kill you and your son."

"Because," Colby continued in the Comanche dialect, "I also know one of your chieftains—Bald Eagle. He and I are brothers. You must know that there is fire in the mind of Bald Eagle when he becomes angry . . . and he would be very, very angry if he learned that you killed his white brother, Sheriff Colby Tucker."

The Indian's dark eyes studied Colby intently, apparently weighing his words. After what seemed an eternity, he spoke. "I am War Bear, also a chief, but Bald Eagle is my leader. We are camped farther downstream." As he spoke, he gestured toward the northeast.

Hope rose in Colby Tucker's breast. "You mean Bald Eagle is camped there with you?"

War Bear nodded, his face solemn and impassive.

"Well, in that case it would be a simple matter for you to talk to him before you kill us," Colby advised, keeping his voice level.

War Bear said nothing. Glaring at Colby with piercing eyes, he grunted, "How is it that you and Bald Eagle are brothers?"

Colby Tucker had dealt with Comanches all his adult life, and he knew that he must impress upon War Bear that he was telling the truth. The Indian was going to have to be convinced that if he killed the Tucker men and stole Libby, he would have to face Bald Eagle's wrath. Thinking fast, Colby replied to the question by asking a question. "Do you know why it is that Bald Eagle is called by that name?"

War Bear immediately replied, "Of course I know, old one. Bald Eagle is called by that name because he has no hair."

"That's right," Colby responded lightly, adjusting himself in the saddle. "He had a terrible sickness when he was a boy . . . and I saved his life. Your leader has called me his white brother since that day." Squinting at the Comanche, the sheriff offered, "I am telling you the truth, but you show me doubt in your eyes."

Without hesitation War Bear mumbled stiffly, "Experience has taught me that whites lie as easily as they speak."

"I'll grant that's true," Colby sighed. "There are many white men who have deceived your people. But if War

Bear will be honest with himself, he knows of Indians who have also spoken with forked tongues."

The subchief growled, "Maybe you lie now to save your white skin."

"Or maybe I am telling the truth. Are you willing to risk facing the anger of Bald Eagle? Life is very sacred to the Comanche, and I saved Bald Eagle's life. If you take mine, you will show Bald Eagle that you do not hold *his* life sacred."

Colby could tell his words were having an effect. He continued, gesturing at Jeff and Libby, "And you will increase your chief's anger if you kill my son and take my daughter-in-law as your squaw."

Jeff and Libby stared at Colby, obviously aware that he was speaking about them, and then gave each other a worried look. The sheriff barely glanced at them in return, not daring to break his stride by turning his attention to them and telling them in English all that had been said. Although War Bear tried to conceal it, Colby saw the trepidation in his dark eyes—but still the Indian did not agree.

"Look, War Bear," Colby said as he pushed back his Stetson, impatience creeping into his voice, "right now I am trailing some very bad men. One of them murdered my other son, and he also murdered my daughter-in-law's mother, father, and brother. If you hold us here much longer, those men are going to get away. I know that the Comanche honor both justice and family—and if those men escape, you will have allowed justice to be defeated and a family to have died unavenged."

War Bear sat impassively for a few moments longer. Then, shaking his head slowly, he declared, "You will come with us to Comanche camp. If Bald Eagle says you speak the truth, then you can go."

Colby was not happy with the decision—but it was a far sight better than dying. He quickly explained to Jeff and Libby what he had prevented from happening—

and also where they were being taken. He cautioned them to remain calm and show no fear. "If we show we are afraid," the sheriff told them, "War Bear may decide it's because we are lying—and not bother taking us to see Bald Eagle."

"I understand, Sheriff," Libby promised, "but I'm confused about why you told him I'm your daughter-in-law."

Colby smiled. "Because Indians have a deep respect for the marriage tie. To them it's the most sacred relationship in life. If War Bear believes you and Jeff are husband and wife, he won't lay a hand on you. But if he knew you're unmarried, my friendship with Bald Eagle wouldn't make a bit of difference." The old lawman did not reveal that if Libby were a widow, she would be freed from the marriage bond. Swallowing his own fear, praying that the Comanche chief would honor their past bond, Colby Tucker told his companions in a voice more confident than he felt, "Don't worry. Once Bald Eagle sees me, the danger will be over."

Eager to get their hands on the money, Harry Blevins and George Niles galloped alongside Duke Malone with great anticipation as they headed straight toward the Red River, to a point east of the town of Roland. The river ran in a southerly direction at this point, past the mouth of the Little Wichita. As the three men raced toward their destination, Blevins and Niles smiled at each other. They had decided that once the money was in their possession, they would ditch Malone at the first opportunity.

Their horses were lathered and gasping for breath as the three outlaws reined in on the west bank of the wide river, in an area thick with heavy brush and tall trees. Malone dismounted, and his two companions did the same. Untying the shovel from his saddle, the killer tossed it into Niles's hands, and without speaking, he started walking along the embankment of the slow-moving river.

He stopped on a grassy ridge and looked around, and Blevins asked, "Trying to get your bearings, Duke?"

"Nope. I know exactly where I am—and where the money is."

Niles's face broke into a broad grin. "Great! Tell me where to start digging."

Malone pivoted and eyed him. Sneering viciously, he finally replied, "Anywhere you want."

Niles looked sharply at Blevins, and then the two men regarded Malone curiously. Before either of his cohorts could question him, Malone whipped out both revolvers and cocked them, training them on the men. "As I said, anywhere you want . . . 'cause it's your own graves you're gonna be diggin'."

Blevins's mouth fell open and Niles's face blanched. It was plain that they saw death looking at them through Duke Malone's demonic eyes.

"I ain't sharin' my loot with nobody," Malone snarled. "You didn't really think I'd be doin' that, did you?" He cackled and added, "You boys must be even dumber than I thought."

George Niles dropped the shovel, desperately grabbed at Blevins's arm, and the two men started backing away. "But we helped you break out of prison!" Niles sobbed.

"That was *your* mistake," chuckled Malone, his mouth a mocking sneer.

"I don't understand, Duke," Blevins groaned. "Why'd you wait till now?"

Keeping pace with the two, holding his guns steady, Malone answered, "I needed your guns in case there was trouble—especially after we heard about them Comanches bein' on the prowl. But I don't need you no more; I can dig up the money all by myself. And after I finish off that rat in Wichita Falls, I'll head someplace where I can live like a king for the rest of my days."

Teetering on the edge of the riverbank, Niles begged, "Please, Duke, don't kill us! Just take the money and go! We don't care about it, do we, Harry?"

Blevins reacted blindly. Undoubtedly knowing his chances of survival were all but nonexistent, he had nothing to lose by going for his revolver, and his hand dipped downward. His fingers had barely reached his gun butt when Malone pulled the triggers, blasting each man off his feet and down the embankment.

Dashing to the edge, Malone watched Harry Blevins's lifeless body hit the water. It momentarily disappeared under the surface, then bobbed back up and began floating away. George Niles lay faceup on the riverbank with his legs in the water. He was still breathing.

Laughing mirthlessly, the killer slid down the short embankment and stopped just short of Niles's head. He looked into the man's eyes, glassy with pain, and cruelly mocked, "I guess you ain't so soft after all, Georgie boy. Looks like it'll take another bullet to finish you off." Slowly raising his revolver so that the former guard was staring into the barrel, Mad Dog Malone fired again, blasting off Niles's face.

Malone lifted his booted foot and with a shove, sent George Niles into the river, where his body stained the water red on its journey downstream.

Chuckling, the killer reloaded his revolvers before holstering them, then climbed the embankment and made his way to where Niles had dropped the shovel. "It's all yours now, Duke," he told himself aloud. He immediately headed toward a large rock beside a massive cottonwood tree and was about to start digging when he heard the rumble of approaching hooves.

"Damn!" Malone exclaimed. "Somebody heard the shots!" He raced for his horse and was about to leap into the saddle when six Comanches came around the brush at a gallop. Spotting him, they thundered in and surrounded him. Swallowing hard, the killer frantically looked from Indian to Indian, each of whom was carrying a single-shot rifle. One of the Indians—wearing the headband and feathers of a chief—was bald-headed and painted for war.

Unexpectedly the bald chief reined in at a distance of some fifty feet, as did the five warriors who flanked him, and raised his hand in the sign of peace. But Malone did not trust the Indian and was sure it was only a ploy to get him off guard. Thinking fast, the killer tossed aside the shovel and jumped out from behind his horse. He drew his revolvers and opened fire, his aim deadly accurate.

Two of the Comanches were instantly blasted off their horses, while the others dived for cover. The chief's horse took a bullet in the head before he could dismount, and both horse and rider went down, with the weight of the animal pinning the lower part of Bald Eagle's body to the ground.

Taking advantage of the confusion, Malone leaped onto his horse and galloped away, with the remaining three able-bodied Comanches firing their rifles in vain. They had not yet reloaded when Malone disappeared through the brush and sped off.

Telling himself he would have to come back for the money later, the killer raced in a frenzy for civilization. Bypassing Roland, which lay in the direction from which he thought the Comanches had come, he made straight for Wichita Falls, where he was sure to find his final victim—Hans Brummer.

Spurring his mount savagely, the wind whipping his face, Malone looked back to see if the Comanches were following, but so far there was no sign of them. *Smart thinkin', killin' that chief's horse,* he told himself. *Them Comanches ain't gonna leave him pinned like that, so that should give me a good enough lead to reach Wich-*

ita Falls. Ain't no way they'd take on a whole town just so's they can come lookin' for me.

The Comanches thundered over the Texas hills, in the direction the killer had taken, for nearly an hour before catching sight of him headed for Wichita Falls. They lashed their horses to get maximum speed, but they were not able to catch him before he reached the outskirts of the white man's domain.

Bald Eagle and his men reined in their mounts a mile from the edge of the town. The ponies blew and snorted as the furious Indians sat silently watching until the killer disappeared from sight among the buildings of Wichita Falls.

The chief's face was dark with rage. Speaking in measured cadence, he ordered, "We will hide near the four corners of the town. Sooner or later the white devil will show himself. When he does, we will capture him and take him to camp." Raising his arms, he declared, "The white killer broke my declaration of peace; for that he will be slowly tortured to death with these hands!"

Knowing he was safe within the confines of Wichita Falls, Duke Malone soon forgot about the Comanches as he rode down the main street, intent on finding Hans Brummer's lawyer brother. He would torture the man if he had to, but when he left this town, he was going to know where to find his traitorous partner.

Tired of looking from one storefront to another, squinting at the names on small signs and trying to find the lawyer's office, Malone decided to expedite his search. He spotted two elderly men chatting in front of a bank, and angling his horse in their direction, he drew up to them. "Afternoon," he said in his most sincere voice. "I was wonderin' if maybe you gents could give me a little information."

One of them peered intently over his spectacles at the killer as if trying to gauge his character. Finally he answered, "What d'you need to know, sonny?"

"I'm lookin' for a friend of mine. Name's Brummer. He's supposed to be livin' here in your town. You know him?"

"Well, yeah. I know two Brummers," the old man admitted with a nod. "Which one's your friend—Hans or Helmut?"

Malone's pulse quickened. "Uh . . . uh . . . Hans. Hans Brummer."

Gesturing with his thumb farther along the street, the old man declared, "Well, I'd imagine at this time of day he'd be at his store."

Malone's eyebrows arched. "His store?"

Leaning slightly in Malone's direction, the old man suddenly looked suspicious. Narrowing his eyes, he demanded, "You mean to tell me you're a friend of his, and you don't know he owns the hardware store?"

"Well, you see, I ain't seen him for six years, and we sorta lost sight of each other." Touching the brim of his hat, Malone smirked. "Thanks for your time. You don't know what a help you've been, mister."

Leading his horse slowly along the street, Malone felt his excitement mounting as he looked from one side of the street to the other for his target. In the third block he saw it: BRUMMER HARDWARE. *Looks like you've been delivered right into my hands, Hans, my friend,* he thought, pulling up in front of the store. The killer dismounted, quickly looped the reins around the hitch rail, gave a quick glance up and down the street, and strode across the boardwalk, entering the store.

My luck's holdin', he told himself, still holding on to the door. *Ain't no customers here.* He sauntered along the aisle toward a young clerk standing behind the counter in the middle of the store. Pretending that he was there to buy something, Malone scanned the shelves laden with tools and hardware.

"May I help you find what you need, sir?" the young clerk inquired, coming out from behind the counter and over to his "customer."

Picking up a hatchet, Malone looked it over, weighing it in his hands. Without warning he strode over to the young man and struck him a sharp blow on the head with the flat of the blade. As the clerk slumped soundlessly to the floor, Malone hurried back to the door and locked it, then flipped over the CLOSED sign in the window.

Drawing his gun, he stealthily made his way to the back of the store, where he could hear someone shuffling papers behind the door marked OFFICE. *That's got to be Brummer*, Malone decided. Raising his foot, he kicked the door open so violently that it slammed against the wall and bounded back. A stout woman was seated behind a desk, and she shrieked loudly, throwing her hands to her face.

Malone shoved his way into the room and looked around, grunting, "Where's Hans, lady?"

The stout woman gasped, "Who are you?"

Grimacing in anger, Malone snapped, "I asked you where Hans is!"

A look of terror washed over the woman's face. "Y-you're Duke M-Malone, aren't you?"

"Oh, you know me, eh? How do you know me?"

"I . . . I'm Hans's wife, Margaret. But he's not here. I . . . I mean he's out of town. He's in Chicago. He won't be home for weeks."

Holstering his gun, the killer grabbed Margaret by the arm and snarled, "You're lyin'! You're just tryin' to protect that stinkin' rat! Now you tell me straight, lady: *Where is he?*"

Margaret's fleshy jaw sagged and she gasped for breath.

"P-please, Mr. Malone"—she shuddered—"I'm telling you the truth. Hans is in Chicago."

His revenge unfulfilled, Mad Dog Malone felt his anger surge through him like a turbulent, storm-swollen river. Swearing loudly, he grabbed Margaret Brummer's throat with both hands and pressed with all his might, crushing her windpipe. Her eyes bulged as she fruitlessly fought against his brutal determination.

The heartless killer choked the life from Margaret Brummer, then threw her body on the floor. Standing over her and breathing hard, he muttered, "I guess I gotta change plans again. I'll go back to the river and get me my money, then hightail it outta these parts. Maybe I'll head into Oklahoma and hole up someplace safe. One of these days I'll come back and get Brummer. There ain't no way he's gonna get away from me—it's just a matter of time."

Malone hurried toward the front of the store. As he passed the clerk, still unconscious, he picked up the hatchet lying near the young man and used it to crush the youth's skull. Then he went to the front door and opened it, casually exiting like any ordinary customer. He left the CLOSED sign in place, figuring that way the bodies would not be discovered for a while—giving him time to make his escape. He mounted up, and moments later he was at the edge of town, heading east toward the Red River. Lashing his horse, he forced it into a gallop. It was already late afternoon, and he wanted to have the money in his hands before sundown.

Intent on getting back to the Red River, Mad Dog Malone had not noticed the four Indians who had followed him for some time at a discreet distance. After a while Bald Eagle and his warriors were sure that the white man was heading back to the spot where the shooting incident had occurred, and knowing a short-cut, they veered off the trail to reach the river ahead of him. They would be waiting for him when he arrived—and he would soon be very sorry he had ever been born.

Arranging themselves in the brush, the Comanches waited patiently. Now their patience was rewarded as the white man appeared, and after briefly looking around, he dismounted. He looked up at the sky, as if determining the time of day, then walked over to where his shovel still lay. He bent to pick it up, and Bald Eagle signaled to his braves.

The Indians burst from the bushes, rifles leveled, and the killer's head jerked up. His face ashen, he put up his hands, apparently realizing that he was a dead man if he went for his guns. There was no way he could draw fast enough to beat four bullets. Knowing the man was trapped, Bald Eagle smiled smugly.

The chief's black eyes bore into the captive's. Folding his hands across his chest, he railed in English, "Do not move, white devil! Put your hands above your head!"

When his command was obeyed, the chief asked, "What do they call you, white man?"

"M-Malone. Duke Malone."

"Well, Duke Malone, you have behaved most stupidly —the first time when you ignored my declaration of peace and killed two of my warriors . . . and the second time when you returned here."

Stepping close, Bald Eagle looked Malone up and down. He abruptly reached out and unbuckled the gun belt from the killer's waist and held it up for inspection. Removing a revolver, he turned it in his hand. He had seen white men use such weapons many times, and he envied the speed and ease of firing that these weapons allowed. While sweat beaded his prisoner's brow, the chief holstered the revolver and strapped the gun belt around his own waist. Bald Eagle then drew both revolvers and cocked them, pointing them at Malone.

"How would you like to die by your own guns, white devil? I assure you, you can believe Bald Eagle when he says the moment will come when you will beg to die this way. And who knows? Possibly that is the way you will welcome death in the end."

The Comanche chief instructed his braves to bind their captive hand and foot, then belly him over his horse's back and lash him to the saddle. After they had done as commanded, the warriors swung onto their pintos and waited for their chief to do likewise. Striding over to the killer's horse, Bald Eagle lifted his prisoner's head by his hair and gazed into his terrified face. Satisfied that Duke Malone knew the fate that awaited him, the chief leaped onto his horse and led his band toward their camp, with Malone's horse in tow.

Chapter Eleven

The sun began to set, and at the Comanche camp on the Little Wichita River, Colby Tucker, Jeff Tucker, and Libby Malone waited fearfully on blankets inside a large tepee. Contrary to what Colby had hoped, Bald Eagle was away from the camp when War Bear brought in his three prisoners, and although the subchief did not bind them, he forced the travelers to remain under guard, awaiting Bald Eagle's return, with four braves standing watch at the tepee to make sure they did not escape.

Trembling uncontrollably, Libby sat with her knees drawn up and her face buried against them. Jeff, his arm around her, held her tightly to him. Watching his young companions, Colby regretted that he had not been more forceful in insisting he hunt for Mad Dog Malone by himself.

"Honey, we're going to be fine," Jeff said, attempting to sound hopeful. Turning to his father, he asked, "Isn't that right, Dad?"

Nodding with more confidence than he felt, the sheriff replied, "I'm certain we will. Bald Eagle won't take his old vow to me lightly, I'm sure, and there's no reason to think he won't honor my family along with me."

Squeezing the young woman tighter, Jeff said softly, "Libby, listen to my father. He wouldn't just be telling us that." His voice lowered as he continued, "I'll tell you something else. I intend to make an honest man of Dad."

Libby's head came up. "What do you mean?" she asked in bewilderment, sounding like a frightened child.

Looking first at Colby, then back at Libby, Jeff replied, "Dad said you're his daughter-in-law. Well, maybe this isn't exactly the proper time or place to say this— but I love you, Libby Malone, and I want you to be my wife. And," he added fiercely, "no tribe of Comanches is going to stand in my way!"

Libby's eyes glistened. Flinging her arms around young Tucker, she whispered, "Oh, Jeff, I love you, too!" Clinging tightly to him as he folded his arms around her, she closed her eyes and whispered, "I want you to know that I trust my heart, Jeff. At first I thought I was turning to you because of all the hurt and pain I've had . . . but all my doubt is gone. It is love—true love—that I feel for you."

Feeling slightly embarrassed at being part of such an intimate moment, Colby Tucker shifted and stood up, walking around the tepee. After a few moments when the young lovers released each other, Colby stepped over to them and put his hands on their shoulders. Jeff looked up at his father, and the sheriff was sure that his son was remembering, as he was, their conversation in the hotel room in Decatur. Smiling at the young lawman, Colby wordlessly told him that he no longer had doubts about the bond Jeff and Libby had formed. Like the strong, sensible young woman, Colby Tucker was satisfied that what they felt for each other was real.

Squeezing Libby's shoulder affectionately, the aging lawman told her, "Nothing in a good long while would please me as much as welcoming you into my family, my dear. Don't you worry about these Indians. Just concentrate on all the happy times you and my son will soon have."

"All right, Sheriff. I'll try."

Libby nestled into Jeff's arms. The three travelers talked about their plans for the future as the sun went down and darkness settled over the tepee.

It had been dark for about an hour when Colby, Jeff, and Libby heard all the camp dogs begin to yap, and then excited voices started shouting. The din went on for several minutes before subsiding. Striding over to the tepee's opening, Colby cautiously lifted the flap and peered outside, curious to see what was going on and suspecting that Bald Eagle had returned. In the light of the campfires Colby watched a small procession of returning warriors make its way into the center of the camp, the chief leading them.

The rest of the tribe gathered around Bald Eagle and his three braves as they dismounted. War Bear approached, and after greeting his chief, he pointed to the captive white man draped over the back of his horse and asked, "Who is this?"

Sliding down off his pinto, Bald Eagle stepped over to his prisoner and yanked up his lolling head. After explaining to his subchief what Malone had done, the chief announced, "For murdering Burning Tree and Running Wolf, the white devil will be punished immediately."

Duke Malone groggily pleaded for mercy, but the Comanche chief ignored him, and signaling to several of his braves, Bald Eagle instructed them to remove the killer from his horse and strip him of his clothing.

When he was wearing nothing but his breeches, Malone was dragged to a log rack shaped like an upside-down U, its legs driven into the ground about six feet apart. He was laid over the top of this rack, on his back, and his legs and arms were spread out and tied down, the ropes being pulled so taut as to stretch his body painfully.

When Malone was secured in this helpless position,

Bald Eagle stepped close to him, with War Bear at his
side. "And now you will learn about Comanche justice," the chief assured his captive. Another signal from
the Comanche's hand brought two braves holding burning torches. Grabbing one, Bald Eagle stepped close to
Duke Malone and held it out toward his body. The
killer, already weakened from the ordeal of the trip,
immediately fainted.

Colby Tucker watched with disbelieving eyes, feeling
the rage inside him growing like a prairie fire. Mad
Dog Malone was no more than fifty feet away from him!
The sheriff battled hard to keep his control from snapping like a dry twig. Looking over his shoulder at Jeff
and Libby, he instructed them, "Stay here." Then he
stepped out of the tepee, pushed past the guards, and
dashed over to Bald Eagle, calling his name in the
Comanche tongue.

The chief turned, holding the lighted torch in front of
him. The angry expression on his face changed to one of
surprise.

"My old friend!" he exclaimed. "What brings you to
my camp after all these years?"

Smiling wryly, the sheriff responded, "I was . . . uh,
invited to come by War Bear. It was either that or die.
I don't think he believed me when I told him we were
brothers."

Bald Eagle turned toward his subchief and angrily
demanded, "Is this true?"

War Bear looked submissive. "It is, my chief. I am
most sorry to have caused your brother worry."

Bald Eagle's eyes narrowed. "Why are you holding
my brother captive?"

War Bear looked away from the chief's intense gaze.
"He is white eyes," he said defensively. "Our enemy."

"Did Colby Tucker not tell you he was my brother?"

"Yes," War Bear admitted. "This is why we did not
immediately kill him—in case he was telling the truth."

Stepping between them, Colby assured Bald Eagle, "It's okay. As a matter of fact, you've saved us a lot of trouble."

"Us?" Bald Eagle queried. "You are not alone?"

"No," Colby told him, gesturing back toward the tent. "My son Jeff and . . . and his bride are traveling with me."

The chief grinned with delight. "This calls for a celebration. Come, we will get them and enjoy a feast, and then you may watch while we punish the white-eyes murderer we have taken captive."

Clasping Bald Eagle's arm, Colby said, "I heard you tell War Bear what this man has done to your braves, and it does not surprise me. You see, this man who has done you much harm is the very man we have been following because he has murdered many people . . . including my son Jim."

Bald Eagle stopped short and stared at Colby; then he shook his head sadly. "I am grieved to hear this, old friend. Perhaps you would like to take part in the punishment."

Before Colby could respond, the tent flap opened and Jeff and Libby stepped out. Colby motioned to his son and said in English, "Bald Eagle, you remember my boy Jeff."

The chief smiled and responded in kind. "We played together as children."

Bald Eagle and Jeff shook hands Indian style, then the chief looked appreciatively at Libby and declared, "Jeff Tucker has a very beautiful squaw."

Libby opened her mouth and started to speak, but before she could utter a sound, an ear-splitting cry from Duke Malone pierced the camp. The young woman looked to her right and gasped. A few yards away, Duke Malone was clearly visible in the light of the burning torches with which his tormentors were scorching his flesh.

Looking carefully at Libby's face, the chief asked, "You too know of this man?"

Nodding tightly, Libby murmured, "He killed my mother, my brother, and my stepfather."

"I am sorry for the pain that this murdering devil has caused my white sister. It is good that you have a husband like Jeff Tucker to give you his strength and comfort."

Libby smiled slightly, and she looked lovingly up at Jeff. Turning back to the Comanche and pointing to Duke Malone, she asked coldly, "What will you do to him?"

Hearing English being spoken, Duke Malone raised his head and opened his swollen eyes, looking toward the speakers. His mouth gaped as he beheld the man he believed to be dead by his own hand. Licking his cracked lips, he choked, "T-Tucker! H-how is . . . it possible? I p-put . . . a bullet . . . through your heart!"

The sheriff strode stiffly over to the murderer and glared unwaveringly at him, breathing deeply as he fought to gain control of his fury. Finally he responded, "Take a look at this badge on my chest, Malone. Your bullet made this hole all right . . . but I wasn't wearing it. You murdered my son Jim."

Malone sucked in a shuddering breath. Almost as if he had not heard a word the sheriff said, he pleaded, "Tucker . . . get me out of here. These savages . . . they want to . . . burn my skin off. Please . . . I can't hold out much longer. Please . . . have mercy."

Colby's insides were churning, and he felt his face grow hot. "Mercy, huh? Is that what you want, Malone? Mercy? You mean like you showed your own daughter and son and their mother? Like you showed my son?"

Leaving Jeff's side, Libby walked slowly over to the rack. She looked at her father stretched on the rack and sneered, "You're getting exactly what you deserve, you demented animal! I hope you suffer tenfold for the way you made Mama suffer! And then I hope your torment lasts an eternity!"

Ignoring his daughter, Malone looked past her to the sheriff and cried, "Please, Tucker, you're . . . a lawman! You can't just stand by . . . and let this happen!"

Colby Tucker knew Malone was right. As much as he would have liked to see Jim's murderer die the way Bald Eagle had planned it, he knew he must talk the chief into letting him have the killer, to return him to Waco. Duke Malone had broken the white man's law before he had shot down the two Comanche braves, therefore he must be punished by the white man's law.

"Tucker . . . please," Malone whispered hoarsely.

"Shut up!" roared the sheriff. Pivoting, he walked back to the chief and told him, "Bald Eagle, I'm going to have to put a heavy weight on our friendship. I must ask you to release this man into my custody in order that justice be served."

The Comanche leader held Colby's gaze for a long moment, then replied evenly, "Justice is being served, my brother. He will be dead in a matter of hours."

"I know how you feel," reasoned Tucker, "but this man began breaking white man's laws many years ago. He is a fugitive from our state prison, and he murdered the chief of the prison while making his escape. As I told you, he also murdered three members of Libby's family, and another woman besides. And . . . Bald Eagle, he killed my son. I know he took the lives of your two braves, and I am pained by the sorrow that is in your heart. But he murdered my *son*! I am asking you as my brother . . . release him to me. I promise you he will hang. He will know death, and that will avenge the loss of your warriors as well as our own people."

Colby read the answer in Bald Eagle's eyes before it came from his lips. "Because you ask this thing in the name of our friendship, my white brother," the chief replied, "I will grant your request." Turning to War Bear, he ordered, "Cut the white devil loose, but be certain he remains bound and kept under guard. He will be leaving with my friend Colby Tucker tomorrow."

Duke Malone heaved a sigh of relief. "Thanks, Tucker," he said, the relief showing on his tormented face. "I won't cause you no problems . . . you'll see. I'll be glad to go with you, just to get away from these savages."

Regarding the killer coldly, Colby replied, "Save your thanks, Malone. And these people you call savages are merely responding in kind to *your* savagery."

Bald Eagle gave orders that the prisoner was to be given his clothing and removed to the other side of the compound, where two braves would stand guard over him. With that done, the Comanche chief turned to his guests and said, "Come. You will share in a feast in your honor and then spend the night."

Nodding in agreement, Colby Tucker responded, "Your kindness is appreciated, my brother. And it will be good to have the opportunity to talk with you about all that is happening between our peoples."

Over an hour had passed since Duke Malone had been released from the rack, and he was beginning to regain his strength. The grogginess was receding, and he looked around, carefully assessing his situation. He found himself sitting on the ground within a few feet of a crude table where the squaws had prepared the food for the feast. They were now some fifteen feet away, tending the meat being roasted over a blazing fire. Noticing a nearby object glinting in the firelight, Malone peered at it and caught his breath. A long-bladed knife had fallen under the table where the squaws had done their butchering. With rising hope the killer realized that even though his hands were tied in front of him and his ankles were bound, it would be a simple matter for him to grab hold of the knife if somehow the two guards could be distracted for a few brief seconds.

Biding his time, Malone waited patiently. Finally his opportunity came when the meal was over. Three small boys playing together were running in circles and shouting, and they collided with the two guards, causing one of them to drop his rifle. Both men bent to retrieve the weapon, scolding the boys severely. Thrusting out his legs, Malone quickly scraped the knife toward him with the heel of his right boot. By the time the guards had regained their stance seconds later, the deadly knife rested securely inside the killer's boot. Chuckling softly, Malone told himself, *You're gonna be mighty sorry you didn't let them savages kill me, Tucker, 'cause there ain't no way I'm gonna let you take me back to be hanged. I'm gonna get clean away long before we get anywhere near Waco—and this time I'm gonna make damn sure you're really dead . . . and your stinkin' son and my treacherous daughter, too.*

The three travelers lay in their bedrolls inside the tepee. Colby was asleep on one side of the tent, while his son was bedded down a few feet from Libby on the other.

Jeff Tucker lay on his back looking up at the moon through the center opening of the tent, thinking how completely his life had changed in a matter of days. Libby suddenly sniffled, and the young marshal raised his head and looked in her direction. She was lying on her side, facing him, and through the moonlight filtering into the tepee he could see the tears on her cheeks.

Throwing aside his blanket, he crawled quietly to her side. "Hey," he whispered, "we're safe now, honey. Everything is going to be all right."

"I know," she whispered in return.

"Then why are you crying?"

"Just missing Mother, Rob, and Ted."

Jeff crawled closer and laid his cheek against hers. His breath was warm in her ear as he whispered, "Libby, I wish there were some way I could take the pain away."

Cradling his head in her hand, she breathed, "The pain won't ever go away, but you've helped to ease it—and you've given me more happiness than I ever thought was possible."

Jeff kissed her neck tenderly, then looked into her eyes. They gazed lovingly at each other for a long moment before kissing lingeringly. They kissed several more times, then he whispered, "Libby, darling, I love you more than anything in life."

Stroking his face, the young woman murmured, "And I love you just the same, my sweet."

Jeff kissed her again, then said, "Libby, I hope you haven't decided you were being too hasty for agreeing to marry me. I mean, if you've thought it over and have changed your mind, I'll understand. . . ."

"Oh, Jeff," Libby whispered, "don't be silly. You're so right for me, I'm positive of that!"

Jeff grinned at her, then grew serious. "Well, how do you feel about being the wife of McLennan County's sheriff? You've gotten a pretty good idea now of the kind of danger a lawman faces from people like your f—like Duke Malone. Are you sure you're willing to put up with that?"

Cupping his chin in her hands, Libby assured Jeff, "What you want is what I want. And," she added, her voice taking on a lighter note, "I guess if I've managed to survive all that we've been through, I'll be able to survive as the wife of a lawman quite nicely, thank you."

"Without a doubt," Jeff agreed, grinning. "So I take it you still want to marry me?"

"I do."

He laughed softly. "Save that response for the preacher."

Giggling, Libby asked, "When?"

"As soon as we get back to Waco?"

"Not a day later!"

Their kiss was ecstatic and lingering. When they parted, Jeff suggested, "Well, as much as I don't want to leave your side, I guess we'd better get some sleep. We're going to be doing some mighty hard riding for the next few days."

Libby's face grew solemn. "I wish we didn't have to travel with that inhuman monster."

"It'll be over in a few days, honey," Jeff promised. "Malone will go to the gallows—and we will have the rest of our lives together."

Chapter Twelve

Soon after first light Colby Tucker roused his son and Libby Malone, telling them it was time to be on their way. After a quick breakfast Colby walked to the opposite side of the clearing where Duke Malone was being held and directed one of the Comanche guards to remove the rawhide thongs binding his ankles. After doing so, the two Indians escorted Malone across the compound and forced him to mount his horse. The man's hands were still tied in front of him, and with an extra length of rawhide, Colby anchored them to the saddle horn.

While Jeff and Libby mounted up, Colby turned to Bald Eagle and thanked his old friend for the hospitality shown to him and his family. He put his hand on the chief's shoulder and told him, "Our friendship means more to me than ever, my brother. Though we find ourselves on opposite sides in this never-ending conflict between red men and white men, I hope we will always remain friends."

Touching Colby's shoulder in the same manner, Bald Eagle replied in a deep and resonant voice, "It is my desire that we meet again, my white brother. But if the great spirit should not allow us to see one another on this earth, we shall one day walk the long valley and renew our friendship where the sun never sets." Then he signaled to one of his braves, who approached holding in his outstretched hands Malone's gun belt. "Do you wish to take the white devil's weapons, Colby, my friend?"

Shaking his head, the sheriff offered, "Why don't you keep them, Bald Eagle? After all, you're the one who captured this murderous dog, so you should reap this small reward. Besides, I'm going to be retiring just as soon as I've delivered Malone to the hangman, so I won't be needing any weapons." Flicking a glance at the killer, Colby added, "And he sure won't be needing any where he's going." Malone glared at the lawman with such intensity that the sheriff could almost feel the man's hatred boring into his body.

Colby tied Malone's horse's reins to his saddle ring, then climbed onto his horse and with a wave of his hand set off. When the four riders reached the edge of the camp, Colby hauled up and gave his prisoner a hard look. "Okay, Malone, I want you to take me to where that money is buried before we head for Waco. I intend to see that money returned to its rightful owners."

Malone sneered at the sheriff, laughing humorlessly. "You're barkin' up the wrong tree, lawman, if you think I'd help you in any way. If I'm goin' to my grave, that money's goin' with me."

Colby did not respond, merely staring at the killer for a long moment. Then he threw up his hands, declaring, "I see. Well, in that case, Mr. Malone, since you won't cooperate, I'm left with no choice but to leave you with Bald Eagle and his braves."

Duke's face twisted. "You're gonna *what*?"

"I guess if I can't take the money with me when I go home, I won't take you, either. I'm sure Bald Eagle will welcome the opportunity to take his revenge."

Malone paled. "You wouldn't."

Turning his horse around, Colby spurred the animal's sides, and Malone's animal bolted as well at the sudden tug on the reins, snapping Malone's head back.

"All right, all right!" Malone shouted. "I'll take you to the money!"

Reining in his horse, Colby smiled. "That's being far more sensible. Let's face it, Malone," the sheriff continued as he turned his horse back around, "even though you'll die either way, it'll be a lot quicker and far less painful to go at the end of a noose."

It was nearly midday when they reached the spot along the Red River that was so familiar to Duke Malone. Bald Eagle's dead pinto still lay where it had fallen the day before, only now big red ants were crawling over the carcass and green-backed flies swarmed around the bullet hole in its head. Colby, his son, and Libby pulled bandannas over their noses to diminish the strong stench. Near the fallen animal was the small shovel that Malone had discarded in his haste to get away from the Comanches.

The four riders reined in their mounts, and Malone pointed with his chin at the cottonwood tree and the large, flat rock at its base. "The money's under the rock behind that tree. I buried it a couple of feet down."

"Well, now you can unbury it," Colby told him. "We'll watch while you dig it up . . . and you'll have to do it with your hands tied."

Malone protested angrily, but it did no good.

Everyone dismounted, and Colby fetched the shovel, handing it to Malone, while Jeff removed the big flat rock. The Tucker men watched with interest while Malone dug, but at their urging Libby took the opportunity to get away from the frightful scene and take a walk along the riverbank.

Strolling by herself some distance away, enjoying the peaceful, lazy river, Libby found herself wishing that she and Jeff could be alone here. Plucking a lovely blue wildflower, she absently smelled it while thinking that it would be so romantic for the two of them just to sit on the bank, holding hands—far from all signs of violence and death—talking about their future together while watching the river roll by.

Suddenly Libby heard Malone swearing loudly, and his voice yanked her back to reality. She turned to see what had disturbed him so and saw him jabbing the deep hole he had dug with the point of the shovel. Walking closer, she was astonished to see Duke Malone suddenly behaving like a crazy man. He threw down the shovel, screaming and shaking his head violently, and Libby stood as if rooted to the spot, watching the ravings of the killer.

"Somebody stole my money! Somebody stole my money!" Malone roared and stabbed the air with his bound hands. "Somebody found it and took it! Somebody found it and took it! Who could have known?" He spun around, flailing his arms, whirling ever closer to Libby.

Colby grabbed hold of Malone's right arm and shouted above his wailing, "Get ahold of yourself, Malone! Calm down!"

Malone jerked his arm free and threw himself on the ground. He flopped and rolled about on the grass while continuing to swear and scream that somebody had stolen his money.

While they stood and watched in astonishment, the two lawmen shook their heads. Jeff turned to his father and asked, "What are we going to do with him, Dad? He's totally lost his mind."

"Best thing to do," replied the elder Tucker, "is to let him go ahead and throw his fit. A man in his state is as strong as four men. Once he spends himself, we'll load him back on his horse and head for home."

Malone rolled and flopped, his hands flailing from his face to his boots, getting nearer and nearer to Libby, who stood with her hand to her mouth, disturbed by her father's state. Without warning, Malone sprang to his feet, at the same time slipping a knife out of his boot. Before Libby could move or either Tucker could get to him, the killer jumped behind Libby, threw his rawhide-bound wrists over her head, and placed the point of the knife against her throat.

Libby froze with fear, feeling the sharp point pressing against her skin. Colby and Jeff started to move toward them, but they stopped short when Malone shouted, "Take one more step and I'll bury this blade in her throat!"

Libby was terrified. She had no doubt he meant what he said. Her chest tightened, and she found it hard to breathe.

"Throw down your guns and back away!" Malone screamed from just behind her right ear.

The two men looked at each other, hesitating.

Their hesitation angered Malone. Spewing saliva, he bellowed insanely, "I said throw them guns down! If you don't do what I say right now, I'll kill her!"

"Malone, she's your own daughter!" Jeff countered. "You can't—"

"She don't mean nothin' to me!" blared the killer. "She's got three seconds to live if you don't throw those guns down!"

Both Tuckers obeyed, dropping their weapons on the ground.

"Now, back off!" commanded Malone.

They took a half dozen steps backward, their eyes riveted on the crazed killer. Still holding the knife poised and ready to plunge into Libby's throat, Malone demanded, "Untie my hands, girl!"

It took the frightened young woman several minutes to get the rawhide loose from Malone's wrists. When she had finally finished, Malone put her neck in the crook of his left arm and, with the point of the knife just under her chin, dragged her toward the lawmen. Forcing her to bend down with him, he picked up the revolvers one at a time. After tossing the first one into the river, he gripped the second one, thumbing back the hammer. Holding the knife in one hand and the revolver in the other, he released Libby and ordered sharply, "Get over there with your friends!"

Libby's legs were a bit weak, but she stumbled across the grass and stood between the two men. Malone then raised the gun, centering the muzzle on Colby's chest, and hissed, "This time I'll shoot the right man!"

"No!" screamed Libby, leaping in front of Colby and shielding his body with her own.

The sheriff reacted instantly, grabbing her and thrusting her out of the way. In doing so he presented his back to Malone, offering a clear target. But instead of firing, Malone threw his head back and laughed demonically. "Hey, girl, you'd have really been fool enough to take a bullet for him, wouldn't you?"

Forcing her way between the two men, Libby looked scornfully at Malone and pleaded, "Haven't you done enough? You've got your freedom; why don't you just ride away and leave us alone?"

The scars on Malone's face turned white as his anger rose. "What kind of damn fool do you take me for? Just go and leave you alone? You gotta be kiddin', girl!" A sneer curled his lip as he added, "I didn't shoot the sheriff 'cause I just decided I ain't gonna let him die that easy—neither him nor his stinkin' lawman offspring. No, I got me some special plans for him and your boyfriend. Then I got special plans for you." Pointing with the knife toward his horse, he commanded, "Go over there and bring me that length of rope that's hangin' on my saddle."

Fearfully Libby looked at Jeff.

"Go ahead, honey," Jeff told her. "If you don't obey him, he'll probably cut you down on the spot."

"That's good advice, tin star. You're damn right I would," chortled Malone. "Do it now, Libby!"

The hellish glare in Malone's eyes prodded Libby to obey. Never once taking her gaze from him, her insides feeling like butter in a churn, she hurried to the horse and removed the rope. Whatever her demented father had in mind for the Tucker men and herself, she had no doubt it would be horrible. Under her breath Libby prayed, "Oh, God, don't let him do this evil thing. You must stop him!"

Forcing Colby and Jeff to lie facedown on the ground, placing their hands behind their backs, Malone made the terrified young woman hold the rope so he could cut it into two six-foot lengths.

"Okay," he then ordered, "I want you tie 'em up. I'll be watchin' real careful, so don't think you can fool me with loose knots. Tie their wrists up real tight, then run them ropes down and bind up their ankles. Start with your boyfriend."

"Malone," said Jeff, "if you've got to take out your vengeance on Dad and me, okay. But I'm begging you not to hurt Libby."

"I don't rightly care what you want, lawman," Malone replied. "My lovin' daughter don't give a damn about me—and I sure as hell don't give a damn about her."

As Libby knelt down to do Malone's bidding, she suddenly remembered the derringer that Colby Tucker wore inside his gun belt. If only she could get her hands on it . . . Reluctantly she bound Jeff's wrists securely, then tied his ankles. Her fingers trembled as she began on Colby. As she wrapped the rope about his wrists, she breathed in a barely audible whisper, "Derringer! Derringer!"

"Yes," he whispered back, so softly that she alone could hear.

Twice Libby tried to run her hand under Colby's belt, but Libby could tell her father was watching too closely. Sweat beaded her brow while she stalled for time, trying desperately to think of a way to get the gun while tying Colby's hands and feet.

"Make it snappy, girl!" Malone growled. "Your two pals are about to take a swim in the good ol' Red River. You boys think you can swim all trussed up like that?"

The crazed killer laughed wickedly, but the laughter abruptly stopped when a booming voice thundered from behind him, *"Drop the gun and the knife, Duke!"*

Pivoting slightly, Malone maintained his grip on the weapons, holding the cocked revolver on Libby, who was still kneeling over Colby Tucker. "Well, I'll be damned. If it ain't my old pal Hans Brummer," the killer sneered.

The bulky German stepped out from behind a cotton-wood tree, a double-barreled shotgun trained on Malone. "Yeah, Duke. It's me. And I'll tell you one last time: Drop the weapons!"

"Better take a good look, Hans," snapped Malone. "I've got this gun trained square on the girl's back. If I pull this trigger, the bullet'll cut her heart in two."

"I can give you two loads of buckshot, Duke," warned the thick-bodied Brummer.

"Yeah, but I might still be able to squeeze the trigger before it hits me. You willin' to take the chance?"

Hans Brummer's face registered his dilemma. When he hesitated, Malone chuckled drily, then arrogantly yelled, "Looks like we got us an old-fashioned Mexican standoff, Hans!"

"You might call it that, Duke. Because I'm not leaving here till you're dead—and you can't stand there and hold the gun on the girl forever!"

"What's your beef with me, old friend?" Malone asked the German. "It was you that ratted on me. I never turned you in to the law."

Brummer's face purpled. "You've murdered my wife!" he screamed. "I'm going to kill you for that!" Glaring at Malone, he bellowed, "She wired me that you had escaped and told me to stay in Chicago, but I didn't listen to her. I was afraid for Margaret's safety. Turns out I had good reason to be, you scaly-bellied reptile!" As he spoke, Hans Brummer stepped closer to Malone, angling his way between the killer and the river. "I never dreamed you'd still be around here," he continued. "I came out to see if you'd dug for the money and had found it gone." He snorted with bitter amusement. "I was just carrying the shotgun as protection against the Comanches."

Malone looked sharply at Brummer. "How'd you know where I buried the money? The only man on earth who knew was Dick Blair—and he died in a shoot-out with the law right after we buried it."

"You're a liar!" Brummer railed. "That's the story you tell, but I know better. You decided to murder Dick and keep all the money yourself. You shot him and left him to die."

Narrowing his eyes suspiciously, Malone snarled, "There ain't no way you could know that!"

"Oh, but there was. Dick wasn't dead when you rode away, Duke. You should have been more careful. He managed to crawl up to the road. I found him lying there when I was on my way to the hideout, and Dick told me what you had done. He also managed to tell me exactly where to find the money before he died. I figured the money was safe where it was, so I went on to the hideout where I was going to kill you for doing Dick in . . . only I didn't make it. Sheriff Tucker caught me before I got there. After what you had done to Dick, I was glad to turn you in to the law."

Malone's craggy face turned blood red. "What'd you do with the money, you squealin' rat?"

"When I got out of jail, I dug it up and used some of it to set up my own hardware business. The rest of it is safe and sound in The Wichita Falls Bank and Trust Company."

Malone's rage made him act impulsively. Spewing out his words, he stepped toward Brummer and screamed, "You stinkin' scum! I've been waitin' a long time to kill you, and now I want that pleasure more than ever!"

When Libby realized Malone had directed his attention away from her, she quickly slipped her hand inside Colby's gun belt and pulled out the derringer, palming it. Her heart pounding like a trip-hammer, she gripped the pistol firmly and took a deep breath. She knew she would not have time to take careful aim but would have to whirl and fire instantly. Even then, the gun her father was holding on her might end her life. Yet she had no choice. She had to stop the madman, and she had to spare the lives of Jeff and Colby Tucker—and it was now or never.

Pivoting on her knees, Libby brought the derringer around and fired. She had wanted to hit Malone in the chest, but in her frantic state she turned a little too far and the slug slammed the killer in the right shoulder.

Even as the bullet hit him, making him stumble slightly, Malone was able to think fast enough to spin and shoot Hans Brummer. The .45 slug plowed through the German's chest, and the shotgun slipped from his hands. Brummer staggered backward, toppling over the crest of the bank into the river. Buoyed by the water, his body was carried downstream by the slow-moving current.

Out of danger from his old nemesis, Malone turned back to his daughter. Libby was on her feet holding the derringer with both hands, aiming it at Malone's heart. Her eyes wild and her breathing hard, she hissed, "I've still got another bullet—and I won't hesitate to use it if you don't drop that revolver!"

Malone backed away from her, his gun pointed at the ground. "Libby, there's no way you're gonna shoot me again. I'm your father. You may hate me, but you couldn't kill me."

"I said, drop your weapon!" Libby commanded.

Loosening his grip on the revolver, he appeared to comply. But then he unexpectedly raised it up, cocking the hammer. Libby's reflexes were faster than his, however, and she immediately fired the derringer's second barrel, and the slug sent Malone tumbling down the bank. Hearing a splash, the young blonde dropped the derringer and ran to the crest, peering down into the river. Duke Malone was nowhere to be seen.

Wanting to do nothing more than collapse, Libby had to will her legs to hold her up, and she made her way back to Colby and Jeff. Kneeling beside Jeff, she began to untie his hands, but her fingers were shaking so badly that she was having a difficult time and progress was maddeningly slow.

"Did you kill him?" asked Colby, impatiently waiting his turn at being released.

"I must have," Libby assured him, fighting to catch her breath. "I couldn't see him anywh—"

A weird gurgling sound suddenly came from the river, followed by a beastlike roar and a mighty splash. Libby screamed with fright, and her face blanched as she quickly stood up.

"Hurry, Libby!" Jeff Tucker cried. "Get these ropes off me!"

Duke Malone roared again, and ignoring Jeff's pleas, the terrified young woman dashed toward the riverbank. She gasped loudly at the sight of the killer clawing desperately at the riverbank and pulling himself out of the water, blood spurting from his wounds. His eyes were bulging as he screamed in pain and fury. Libby felt as if she were in a nightmare, with Duke Malone some unstoppable beast rising from the depths of the river. Backing away from the edge, her foot struck something hard. She looked down and saw Hans Brummer's shotgun, and her heart pounding, she bent down and picked it up.

Taking a deep breath, she hefted the weapon and walked back to the riverbank. Rigid with determination, Libby yelled down at the man still struggling to climb the bank, "Stop right there!"

His fingers digging into the grassy slope, Malone looked up gasping and slack-featured, staring at the ominous black muzzles of the shotgun trained on his head. "Libby!" he wheezed. "Please don't! I love you, Libby! I love you!"

"*Love!*" she spat bitterly. "You don't know what the word means, you bloody maniac. You were going to kill me right along with the Tuckers, and you know it!"

"No, baby!" he insisted, sobbing. "No, I wasn't, honest! I love you! I wouldn't have killed you!"

"Liar!" she retorted. "You murdered Rob, and he was your son. You would have murdered me without even blinking!"

"No! No, it's different with you than with Rob! I really love y—"

"You're well named," she cut him off. "You're nothing but a mad, rabid dog . . . and there's only one thing to do with a beast that has gone insane!"

Libby's harsh words lit a fire in Malone's wild eyes. Suddenly he lunged upward, kicking and clawing, screaming, *"I'll kill you! I'll kill you! I'll kill you!"*

But Libby set her jaw and, swallowing hard, squeezed the front trigger, blasting the killer's chest. The shotgun was still bucking from the first charge when she pressed the second trigger. Duke Malone's evil face was ripped apart, disappearing in a mass of blood. His body flipped back and hit the water as the echo of the dual blasts ricocheted across the broad river and reverberated along its uneven banks.

Feeling as though a tremendous burden had been lifted from her shoulders, Libby stood there holding the smoking shotgun, her eyes fixed on the river. Her father's body went under, then surfaced, the water around him turning a muddy crimson. Duke Malone's daughter followed her father's lifeless form with her eyes as it drifted slowly away. Her feet and arms were leaden. Slipping unnoticed from her numb fingers, the shotgun tumbled halfway down the riverbank. Tears ran down her face as she stood gazing into the distance and whispered, "Mother . . . Rob . . . Ted . . . it's done. It's over."

Suddenly Libby realized that Colby and Jeff had been calling to her, but their voices only now penetrated her thoughts. Turning slowly around, Libby made her way over to them.

"Libby!" called Jeff Tucker as she drew near. "Thank God you're all right!"

"Untie us, honey," Colby insisted, pulling against the rope.

Moments later the two men were free of their bonds and on their feet. Jeff took Libby into his arms and held her, and she laid her head on his chest, clinging to him.

"If you need to cry, darling," Jeff told her tenderly, "my shoulders are mighty good for that."

"No," she said calmly. "I've cried for Mother, Rob, and Ted. I won't be crying over Malone. I'm glad he's dead. I'm sorry I had to be the one to kill him, but there was no other choice. At any rate, it's done now."

Colby moved beside her and slipped his arm around her as well. "Libby, my dear, I don't quite know what to say. With all you've been through, you still had the strength and courage to do what must have been the hardest thing in the world. My hat's off to you, little gal."

Libby smiled up at the handsome silver-haired man, and she slipped out of Jeff's embrace and into Colby's. He held her close and his voice broke as he choked out, "Libby, words are sort of weak vessels for what I want to say, but they're all I've got. You were willing to take that bullet for me, and as long as I live, I'll never forget it. Thank you, my child."

Libby felt a warm tear on her cheek, and she was not quite sure if it was hers or the sheriff's. "I love you," she said softly. "It's as simple as that."

Colby sniffed and looked at his son, telling him in mock earnestness, "Jeff, don't you think it's time you set a date?"

Libby leaned back and smiled at Colby. "We already have—the day we get back to Waco."

A broad grin spread across Colby's face. Scooping Libby back into his arms, he kissed her forehead and said, "Well, then, we'd better get going. We wouldn't want to keep that preacher waiting, would we?"

"No, sir." Libby laughed. Slipping from Colby's embrace, the young woman took Jeff's hand. "Come, my love. There's a brand new sheriff's badge waiting for you in Waco. Let's go home."

Colby squeezed Libby's shoulder, then turned and walked toward the river.

"Where are you going?" Libby asked curiously.

"Just want to take care of something. You two go on ahead. I'll catch up in a couple of minutes."

Libby and Jeff mounted up and watched while Colby Tucker walked to the riverbank. He stood there for a long moment, gazing at Duke Malone's body bobbing and turning in the middle of the river, about to disappear around a bend a quarter-mile downstream. Pulling the bullet-drilled badge from his shirt, he held it in the palm of his hand and looked at it for a few seconds. Then he gave a mighty heave and tossed the badge far into the river. Turning around, a look both of sadness and contentment on his face, he strode to his horse and swung into the saddle.

"Like you just said, Daughter, let's go home."

**FROM THE PRODUCER OF WAGONS WEST
AND THE KENT FAMILY CHRONICLES—
A SWEEPING SAGA OF WAR AND HEROISM
AT THE BIRTH OF A NATION.**

THE WHITE INDIAN SERIES

Filled with the glory and adventure of the colonization of America, here is the thrilling saga of the new frontier's boldest hero and his family. Renno, born to white parents but raised by Seneca Indians, becomes a leader in both worlds. THE WHITE INDIAN SERIES chronicles the adventures of Renno, his son Ja-gonh, and his grandson Ghonkaba, from the colonies to Canada, from the South to the turbulent West. Through their struggles to tame a savage continent and their encounters with the powerful men and passionate women in the early battles for America, we witness the events that shaped our future and forged our great heritage.

☐ 24650	White Indian #1	$3.95
☐ 25020	The Renegade #2	$3.95
☐ 24751	War Chief #3	$3.95
☐ 24476	The Sachem #4	$3.95
☐ 25154	Renno #5	$3.95
☐ 25039	Tomahawk #6	$3.95
☐ 25589	War Cry #7	$3.95
☐ 25202	Ambush #8	$3.95
☐ 23986	Seneca #9	$3.95
☐ 24492	Cherokee #10	$3.95
☐ 24950	Choctaw #11	$3.95
☐ 25353	Seminole #12	$3.95
☐ 25868	War Drums #13	$3.95
☐ 26206	Apache #14	$3.95
☐ 27161	Spirit Knife #15	$3.95
☐ 27264	Manitou #16	$3.95
☐ 27841	Seneca Warrior #17	$3.95

Prices and availability subject to change without notice.